PURLOINED Poinsettia

DAHLIA DONOVAN

TANGLED TREE PUBLISHING

PURLOINED POINSETTIA

MOTTS COLD CASE MYSTERY BOOK 4

DAHLIA DONOVAN

TANGLED TREE PUBLISHING

The Grasmere Cottage Mystery Trilogy

Dead in the Garden | Dead in the Pond | Dead in the Shop

Motts Cold Case Mystery Series

Poisoned Primrose | Pierced Peony | Pickled Petunia | Purloined Poinsettia

London Podcast Mystery Series

Cosplay Killer | Ghost Light Killer | Crown Court Killer

Stand-alone Romances

After the Scrum | At War With A Broken Heart | Forged in Flood | Found You | One Last Heist | Pure Dumb Luck | Here Comes The Son | All Lathered Up | Not Even A Mouse | The Misguided Confession

The Sin Bin (Complete Series)

The Wanderer | The Caretaker | The Royal Marine | The Botanist | The Unexpected Santa | The Lion Tamer | Haka Ever After

For information, contact the publisher, Tangled Tree Publishing.

WWW.TANGLEDTREEPUBLISHING.COM

EDITING: HOT TREE EDITING

COVER DESIGNER: BOOKSMITH DESIGNS

EBOOK ISBN: 978-1-922679-27-7

PAPERBACK ISBN: 978-1-922679-28-4

A Pineapple, a cat in a sweater, and a turtle hide in a garden in the middle of winter to avoid the clutches of the icy queen ogre.

Right.

Mildly dramatic.

More than mildly dramatic.

After living in Cornwall for almost a year, Pineapple "Motts" Mottley hadn't anticipated returning home for the holidays. Not when home meant her overbearing mother and her mild-mannered, loving father. If it hadn't been for the serial killer trying to complete his schoolgirl collection, she'd have stayed hidden in her little cottage on the top of the cliff above Polperro.

No one knew for certain who the serial killer

was. Or if they were really after her. The police had managed to determine many of the girls in her primary school class had been murdered or died in suspicious circumstances over the past thirty-plus years.

Definitely not a coincidence.

So Motts had resigned herself to spending most of December in her childhood home. With her parents. At forty years old. She was not looking forward to any of it, considering she'd left London for a reason.

To get away from the noise and her mother.

Sometimes the noise is Mum.

Her mother meant well. She just hadn't ever managed to adjust to having a daughter who was autistic, asexual, and biromantic. Motts had hoped at some point she would.

She hadn't.

At least her mother had stopped trying to set her up on dates with unsuspecting men and women. Motts had enough chaos in her life. She didn't need random strangers thinking of her romantically.

She couldn't manage the people she already knew thinking of her romantically.

"Still hiding in the garden after all these years,

poppet?" Her dad came over to sit beside her. "What's she done now?"

"Tried to insist I go carolling with her this evening," Motts grumbled. She lifted Cactus, her beloved Sphynx cat, into her arms to ensure his knitted sweater was on correctly. "First, I can't sing. Second, she's going to try setting me up on a date again. Third, why would I want to parade myself around to a bunch of strangers' houses?"

Her mum simply couldn't grasp that Motts wasn't interested in falling head over heels into a romance. She had enough dating confusion with her friend, Detective Inspector Dempsey Byrne, who might be flirting with her, and Beckett Ferris, who had recently moved to Polperro to be closer to their grandparents and ran a restaurant in the village. They were definitely flirting with her.

"What happened to the Teo chap?"

"Moved to Yorkshire." Motts missed Detective Inspector Herceg. He was lovely. Just not *the one*, whatever that meant. She didn't know if she had a *one*. "We chat via text."

"And Vina?"

"Vina? My best friend? Who I broke up with years ago? Who is in love with a lovely woman?" Motts stared at her father in confusion. Pravina

Griffin (and her brother Nish) were two of her closest mates. They ran a café and bakery with their parents out of Polperro. "I've told you this."

"Never hurts to ask."

Right.

Sometimes it does.

Her father left her to commune with nature. Motts had a blissful moment of peace before the back door opened. She sighed deeply and cuddled Cactus in her arms.

"Pineapple." Her mum came out into the garden, disrupting the chilly calm Motts had been hoping to enjoy. "Aren't you going to get ready for carolling, darling?"

"I'm not interested." Motts had already said "no" multiple times and in varying ways. She stood up with Cactus in her arms and found Moss to take both of them inside the house with her. It was too cold to leave them in the garden. "I'm not going with you, Mum."

"You must learn to socialise."

"I have friends. Good ones. I'm also forty. You're too late to turn me into a social butterfly now." Motts made sure Cactus had his afternoon snack and got Moss back into his massive terrarium. Her dad had gone out of his way to make it the most unnecessarily luxurious home for a turtle that she'd ever seen. "You, my dear, are spoilt. Granddad's taking good care of you."

After settling both Cactus and Moss, Motts grabbed her phone and a thicker cardigan from her bedroom. She had to get out of the house for a little while. And definitely not with her mum and her carolling friends.

"Where are you going, darling?" Her mum caught up to her at the front door.

"For a walk." Motts rushed out the door before her mum could ask any further questions. "Holy mother of mittens. She's going to drive me batty. Completely and totally."

Being in her childhood home was as annoying as Motts had feared it would be. She'd moved out later than most people she knew, in her late thirties. She owed it to her auntie bequeathing her the cottage in Polperro.

Would I still be here if she hadn't? I hope not. Can I go home now?

Probably not.

Ruddy rude rudeness ruins rebellious rewards.

Not my best work.

Heading toward the corner at the end of the street, Motts stumbled to a halt, almost tripping over a crack in the pavement. *Pale blue car.* It was like a mirage had followed her all the way from Cornwall.

It sat across the way. Parked down the road, they had a perfect view of her front door. No matter how hard Motts tried, the glare off the windshield prevented her from seeing the driver's face clearly.

There have to be loads of pale blue Nissans in London. Right? It can't be the same one stalking me all the way from Cornwall.

Yet, it looked eerily similar to the one that had followed her around Polperro for weeks. Gathering her nerves, Motts crossed the road and continued toward the Nissan. The car immediately began reversing away from her.

Motts kicked herself for not getting her phone out more quickly to take a photo. She eyed her phone for a moment. "Should I tell Dempsey?"

Detective Inspector Dempsey Byrne handled cold cases. *Technically DCI: Detective Chief Inspector Byrne. Fancy.* He had a team of investigators working out of London on crimes committed at least twenty years ago. One of them involved the murder of Jenny, Motts's best friend from primary school.

Her only friend at the time.

In the past year, Dempsey had been attempting to solve Jenny's case. He'd managed to uncover a prolific serial killer who'd murdered their way through the majority of the girls in her class. Aside from Motts, there were only three other survivors.

Two in America.

One in Australia.

Thirteen dead in suspicious circumstances.

I should text him.

Motts: Remember the pale blue Nissan in Cornwall? The one you suspected might be connected to Jenny's killer?

Dempsey: I do. Never did find anything connecting the owner—a sweet little old woman from Norwich who lent her car to a friend's son. Couldn't find either the friend or son.

Motts: I'm 85% certain I saw it down the street from my parents' place.

Dempsey: Are you outside?

Motts: How else would I see a car parked down the street?

Dempsey: Please go inside.

Motts: The driver took off when I approached. I couldn't see their face.

Dempsey: I'll be there within the hour. Traffic allowing. Please go inside.

Motts: But my mum's inside and driving me up the wall. Not literally. But still.

Dempsey: If you go inside, I promise to take you out for a quiet adventure.

Motts: Can an adventure be quiet?

Dempsey: Do you want to be pedantic or have an enjoyable moment away from your mother?

Motts: I can't do both?

Fresh air in London definitely didn't do the same for Motts as it had in Cornwall. So she decided to cut her losses and retraced her steps back home. Her mum was waiting for her—all dressed up for her evening carolling.

"You should come with, darling."

Motts wondered if there was an Indian deity dedicated to patience. She'd have to ask Vina or Nish; maybe they could make an offering for her. "I would rather destroy all of my origami creations than inflict myself on random strangers in the name of holiday spirit. Carolling causes casualties."

With her mother momentarily stunned by her

omission, Motts made her way through the house to her room. She found Cactus curled up in the centre of the bed. He seemed mildly subdued.

Her cottage had offered Cactus more freedom. Her cat generally tried to avoid her mum as much as Motts did. *Maybe great minds do think alike.*

"Pineapple, darling." Her mum had followed her through the house. But, unfortunately, it was always jarring to hear her full name. Just about everyone else in her life called her Motts. "Why must you be so difficult? Off the bed, Cactus. You'll get fur everywhere."

Same, Mother, same. Why must you be so difficult?

I am forty years old. I am in perimenopause. When are you going to stop attempting to arrange my life to sort the fantasy in your mind?

"He's naked. He can't get fur everywhere." Motts wanted to bury her face into a pillow and scream. But, technically, Cactus wasn't naked. He had a sort of peach fuzz over his body along with his knitted sweater. "And I can't go out. I've a friend coming over."

"A friend? What friend?"

Motts hesitated. She knew exactly how her mother would react to a man coming over to see her. "DCI Byrne."

"Is he, darling?"

Motts groaned internally. She could already see the matchmaking happening in her mum's mind. And it definitely involved wedding bells, frilly dresses that Motts would never wear, and hideously tacky decorations. "He wants to discuss Jenny's case."

"He shouldn't bother you with such troublesome things. You're delicate."

"I've delicately stumbled upon three dead bodies thus far without swooning into a state of incomprehension. I think I can manage a conversation about a thirty-something-year-old cold case." Motts felt the surge of anxious energy coming that usually signalled an impending meltdown. "Do you mind? I want to shower before he arrives."

Dodging her mum with a deftness born from years of practice, Motts disappeared into her en suite with a sigh of relief. She grabbed a stack of towels and screamed into them, trying to release some of the overwhelming tension bombarding her mind.

She dithered about in the bathroom for thirty minutes. Longer than necessary. The shower ran despite her not getting into it. She'd already bathed that morning. Twice in one day seemed excessive.

Motts stared at her tired bluish-grey eyes in the

mirror over the sink. Her face was paler than usual, another sign of how much the stress of being home was affecting her. She shoved her brown hair up out of her face with a sigh. "Pull yourself together. You can do two weeks with Mum and Dad. It won't kill you."

"Motts? Your friend is here. You might want to rescue him from your mum." Her dad knocked on the closed door, jolting her out of her thoughts.

Bugger.

Rushing out of her room, Motts darted past her father. She found Dempsey in the sitting room with Cactus ensconced on his shoulder. Typical. Her cat had a thing for detective inspectors.

He'd befriended two of them. Both tall. Both broad-shouldered. Dempsey had a few years on Teo, though. His salt-and-pepper hair and beard made him a bit of what her cousin River called a silver fox.

"Hello." Motts came to a stop in the middle of the room. Dempsey seemed utterly unbothered by the rapid-fire invasive questions her mum flung at him. "Fancy a stroll around the garden?"

"How about we step out for a while?" Dempsey countered. He had her out of the house before either of her parents could comment. "Delightful woman."

"Don't they teach you how to lie better in the

police?" Motts waited for him to unlock his Range Rover. She climbed into the passenger seat and felt some relief at being out of the house. "Did I say hello?"

Dempsey reached into the back seat and retrieved a set of noise-cancelling headphones. "Got a spare pair of these for myself. Why don't you pop these on? Enjoy some quiet while I drive us."

"You bought two pairs of noise-cancelling headphones?"

"Yes." He was completely unperturbed by her bewildered stare. "Go on, then. We can chat in a bit."

"You're genuinely the oddest police detective I've ever met."

"Thank you." Dempsey winked at her. "How many have you met?"

"Including you?" Motts eased the headphones onto her head. "Four?"

"I'm odder than Herceg?"

Motts nodded immediately. "Less shouty eyes, though."

"DI Herceg has shouty eyes?" Dempsey chuckled.

"Yours twinkle like you're about to tell me a joke that I won't understand." Motts reached up to switch on the noise cancelling. "So yes, far less shouty."

CHAPTER TWO

"My mum wanted me to go carolling." Motts spoke after enjoying the blissful, cushioned silence of the headphones for almost twenty minutes. "Carolling. Me."

"Are you protesting the concept overall or her audacity in attempting to coerce your involvement?" Dempsey had been driving them around Dulwich, the village in London where her parents lived. "Do people actually still go carolling?"

"Apparently."

"Sounds torturous at best." Dempsey grimaced. "Why inflict objectively dreadful singing on the unsuspecting public?"

"Did you eat another thesaurus since I last saw you?" Motts made sure to smile so he'd know she was only joking. She never quite knew if someone would pick up on her teasing. And she'd made the mistake of taking someone seriously when they'd been taking the mickey often enough herself. "Or perhaps an entire collection of books by some forgotten author?"

"I'm loquacious by nature."

"Loquaciously lists luscious lyrical… words." Motts considered all the L-words she could think of for several seconds while Dempsey laughed beside her. "Lexeme!"

"Pardon?"

"Loquaciously lists luscious lyrical lexemes," Motts repeated triumphantly. She grabbed her phone to make sure she'd gotten the right word. "I suppose lexicon would work just as well."

"You take your alliterations quite seriously."

Motts eyed him for a moment, unsure if he was making fun of her. He'd never done so in the past, so she figured he wouldn't now. "I find them satisfying."

"Maybe you need the thesaurus then. To help you find the best words for your own personal lexicon." Dempsey stopped at a red light. "Fancy fish and chips or something else?"

"Are we having dinner?"

"We are. Dinner and discussion. You're going to

tell me all about the pale blue Nissan. Well? What do you fancy?"

"Fish and chips." Motts had eaten quite a few salads and healthy meals in the past five days. Since her return from Cornwall, her mum was on one of her "my daughter must consume a specific diet because it might help her function" kicks. It didn't help. At all. Mostly Motts found it irritating. "Chips. All the chips. Greasier the better, with loads of ketchup."

"Why am I sensing a story in your sudden craving?"

"My mum." Motts shrugged.

"Is she opposed to chips?" Dempsey seemed suitably horrified at the idea.

"My mum has this confused idea that changing my diet will somehow change the way my mind works." Motts gripped her hands together in her lap. She stared out the window, trying not to get emotional. The past five days had been exhausting, and most of it had been spent burying her feelings to get by. "As if eating only healthy foods will magically turn me into a normal human being."

"Motts." Dempsey reached out and gently pried her hands apart. "You're going to hurt yourself. And I hate to break it to your mum, but no one is normal.

I've seen just about every kind of person as a copper. No such thing as *normal.*"

"She has ideas of what her perfect daughter was supposed to be." Motts gestured to herself. "And this isn't it."

"Her loss. Not yours. You are brilliant, funny, and clever. Sod whatever made-up image anyone else tries to impose on you." He squeezed one of her hands, then let go of her. "Even your mother. Now, are we sure fish and chips are going to do the job? I'm open to picking up the greasiest, most unhealthy meal I can think of."

"Chips." Motts thought any number of hurts could be cured with salty, greasy potato goodness.

"Chips it is." Dempsey grinned.

Making his way through the afternoon traffic, Dempsey pulled up outside one of the local chippies. He went inside to get their order, leaving her to soak up the silence. Motts eased her phone out of her pocket to text in the group chat.

About her mum.

About Dempsey.

And about the pale blue car.

The group chat consisted of Pravina; her twin brother, Anish; and Motts's younger cousin, River. Nish and River had been dating for several months now. They'd all known one another since childhood, though.

Motts: Pale blue car followed me from Cornwall. Mum is still on her salad kick. Might actually lose my mind. And Dempsey's taking me out for chips.

Vina: Are you on a date with the silver fox?

Motts: Not a date. Don't think it's one.

River: Definitely a date. She never knows. We can't take her word. Bet she'd be halfway down the aisle to getting married without realising someone was flirting with her.

Motts: Not getting married. Not on a date. And are we genuinely focused on THAT and not the creepy stalker who found me in London?

Nish: 1. We can't do anything about the PBC. 2. We've all decided to visit you for Christmas so you'll have back-up in dealing with your mum.

Vina: We'll be there in the morning since

we're spending the night in Brighton. Mum and Dad are minding the café.

Motts: You don't have to.

Vina: Yes, we do. What sort of friends would we be if we didn't?

Nish: Plus her girlfriend, Taara's in London for the holidays.

While the twins argued back and forth in the group chat, Motts pocketed her phone for a bit. She wondered if the rest of the family were coming up for the holidays. Auntie Lily usually insisted that the Chen-Mottley crew spend Christmas together, so River wouldn't come up to London without his parents. She wondered if they were closing their brewery for the holidays.

Not for Christmas.

The Griffins were a little less holiday obsessed. Cadan and Leena usually spent December relaxing. However, they occasionally went to India to celebrate the anniversary of when the Cornish cricketer had stumbled upon his Bollywood beauty so many years ago.

Rechecking her phone, Motts found the argument still going. She rolled her eyes. The twins loved to bicker with each other while River periodically prodded at them.

"Have they decided if this is a date?" Dempsey asked with a mischievous twinkle in his eyes when he returned to the vehicle, proving how well he'd come to know her friends.

"They haven't reached a consensus." Motts inspected the food packet he handed over to her. She assumed Dempsey was joking. He couldn't possibly be interested in a date. Not with her. "We're friends."

"We are," Dempsey agreed with a grin. "Tell your friends when it's a date, there won't be any room for confusion. Why don't we drive to the park to eat? We can talk about why you shouldn't walk toward serial killers in pale blue cars."

"I don't even know if that's who was driving. You've never found the vehicle."

"And yet it keeps finding you," Dempsey grumbled. He sounded incredibly irritated. "Just be careful."

"I am always careful." Motts carefully avoided glancing in his direction. "Mostly. Danger finds me no matter how cautiously I attempt to sidestep it. Have you had any breaks in Jenny's case?"

"Not Jenny specifically."

"But?" Motts prompted when he fell silent.

"We've identified the two brothers you remembered. Jonty or Jonathan and Hugo Barbrow." Dempsey had her immediate attention.

She'd mentioned the brothers to him when he'd first questioned her about Jenny's case what felt like ages ago. They'd stood out to her. The older of the Barbrows had often stood on the corner and harassed the girls in her class.

"Barbrow?"

"Their grandfather was apparently from Sweden." Dempsey glanced over when she snuck a chip out of the packet. "Save me a few."

"So Jonty and Hugo?" Motts refused to be distracted.

"Jonty was indeed the younger of the two. Hugo got himself kicked out of several schools before his mum decided to educate him at home." Dempsey found a parking space with a good view of the park and eased into it. "And before you ask, he was politely asked to leave for demonstrating antisocial behaviour."

"I'm antisocial."

"You're an introvert who is uncomfortable around strangers. Hugo Barbrow made a habit of destroying the property of others. Jonty joined him on some of his misadventures." Dempsey grabbed his packet of chips and fish when she held the bag out to him. "We've managed to find a number of police reports about vandalism and missing pets around their home. Nothing was ever proven."

"Do either of them have a pale blue Nissan?"

"No idea." Dempsey shrugged.

"Isn't London the most watched city in the world? How can you not know?"

"Despite what the police would like people to think, we are not omniscient."

"Shouldn't that be omnipresent?"

"We're neither." Dempsey popped a fry into his mouth. "I certainly wouldn't want to know everything or be everywhere. Sounds exhausting. I'm tired enough from what I am aware of."

Is it omniscient or omnipresent?

Probably doesn't matter.

"Seriously, though, can't you do a search for what cars they own?"

"Allow me to clarify." Dempsey waved a chip at her, sending salt flying. "We've identified the vehicles legally owned and registered to the Barbrow brothers. Unfortunately, we've yet to find a connection between them and a lowly Nissan."

"Lowly?"

"They've transformed themselves from hooligans

in and out of trouble to wealthy toffs. Something to do with inheriting money after their parents died about ten years ago." Dempsey paused to finish up his chips. "They were left the house, cars, and a successful business that they sold before their parents were cold in the ground."

"How'd they die?" Motts found it odd both parents passed away at the same time. "An accident?"

"Industrial fire at one of their warehouses." Dempsey glanced out of the window at a vehicle passing in front of them. He watched for a few minutes before returning to the conversation. "And yes, I'm aware how suspiciously convenient that is."

"Suspiciously salacious sabotage." Motts considered briefly then continued. "Sablefish."

"Sablefish?"

"First word that popped into my mind."

"Sablefish was the first word that popped into your mind after 'suspiciously salacious sabotage'?" Dempsey chuckled. "Your mind is always a wonderful journey."

"What do you know about the industrial incident?" Motts had experienced her own close call with a fire. She'd been investigating a woman's death at a brewery when the killer had set the warehouse ablaze. It had been a near miss, with her having to leap from a second-floor window. "Actually, maybe I don't want to know about it."

Dempsey turned to her seriously. "Still having nightmares about the fire?"

"Occasionally."

"I can recommend a therapist who deals with post-traumatic stress if you want." Dempsey offered her the remnants of his chips, since she'd already scarfed down her own. "They do phone visits, so you wouldn't even have to go in person."

"I'm all right."

"As long as you know it's perfectly fine not to be all right." Dempsey frowned while staring out the window again.

"What?" Motts tugged the seat belt a little to allow her to lean forward to see what had caught his attention. "You've gone all… detective-y."

"Not a word."

"Might as well be." Motts didn't see anything out of the ordinary. "You've an air of the police about you."

"I always have an air of the police about me. I am the police." Dempsey carefully gathered up what was left of his meal. He bundled it up and returned it to the bag. "Seat belt on?"

"Yes." Motts tugged on it for a second time to demonstrate. "You're worrying me."

"That car was parked three houses down from yours. Then saw it again when I picked up our dinner. Now it's suddenly here?" Dempsey grabbed his phone and made a call.

While Motts listened in, Dempsey called who she assumed was one of his fellow detectives. He asked them to trace the registration of the vehicle. She wondered how he'd even noticed what was parked near her parents' place.

She hadn't. The pale blue Nissan had been foremost on her mind, not other vehicles. It had followed her from her cosy cottage, after all.

It made sense for the killer to use more than one vehicle. They were clever, whichever of the Barbrow brothers it was. Maybe they'd both been involved.

Are we being too focused on them?

Who else could it have been, though?

All her teachers would be too old, surely, to be continuing to kill. To travel around the globe, hunting down former schoolgirls

Travelling.

Travelling.

Travelling?

"Dempsey?" Motts found a thought suddenly

occurring to her. "How is the killer managing to slip in and out of another country after committing murder without being noticed? Has either of the Barbrows been to Australia and New Zealand recently? Been near any of the suspicious deaths?"

"Both frequently travel for business. Along with one other suspect we've had our eye on. Unfortunately, the local authorities were unable to find definitive proof of any of them." Dempsey dropped his phone onto the dash. "I'm going to take you home."

"To see if we're followed?" She took his silence as an affirmative. "At least Mum should already be out carolling."

"Motts?" His usually twinkling brown eyes had turned serious. "If you need a break while you're in London, send me a text, all right? No point in you suffering through the holidays. Or, at all, really."

Arriving home, Motts stared up at the familiar two-storey dwelling. Dempsey had driven off once she'd made it to the door. Her mother would hopefully be gone most of the evening.

This isn't home.

Not anymore.

"Are you home, poppet?" Her father poked his head out of his study.

"No?" Motts bent down to lift Cactus, who'd been waiting by the door for her. "I am a figment of your imagination."

"A figment with good timing. Your mother's off for the evening. Want to listen to records with me?" Her father gestured over his shoulder into his study.

"Not tonight." Motts buried her face in Cactus's little sweater.

Saying a quick good night, Motts made her way upstairs to her old bedroom. She hated the way being in London was so suffocating. It did show a stark contrast to how much she'd grown in Cornwall.

In London, even in her thirties, Motts had hidden at home more often than not. She rarely ventured beyond Dulwich. In Cornwall, she'd ridden her bicycle and Vespa all around Polperro.

The move had been the right decision to make. She'd found freedom. Found herself, really, as trite and clichéd as that sounded.

London was temporary.

She wasn't going backwards.

Despite the freezing weather, Motts had retreated to the garden almost immediately the following morning. Her mother was in rare form. She'd insisted on an egg white omelette for breakfast.

It was bland.

And boring.

And not lemon curd on toast.

If Motts wasn't popping by Griffin Brews for a breakfast pasty of some sort, she tended to eat the same thing every morning. Lemon curd on toast with either tea or coffee. Her mother had a no-sugar version that tasted dreadful.

Like having a mouthful of gelatinised Lemsip, which was neither pleasant nor enticing.

Nothing says good morning like jellied lemon cough syrup.

Motts stared mournfully at the date on her phone. *December twenty-first. Is it too late to go home for Christmas?* Cactus leapt up into her lap. "Hello there. Have you chased down Jack Frost yet?"

Meow.

"Yes, I'm aware this is nowhere near as comfortable as your garden in Cornwall." Motts petted his head. She'd have to take him inside soon. The weather was too chilly for his delicate sensibilities. "Shall we see what kind of snacks I have hidden in my luggage? Maybe a little catnip to get you through the day?"

Meow.

Stepping into the house, Motts veered away from the stairs and toward the front door when someone rang the doorbell repeatedly. She found a boisterous Vina and a frowning Nish waiting for her. Cactus immediately went to greet the twins.

"Long drive?" Motts glanced between the siblings.

"Someone"—Nish turned slowly to glare at his sister—"and by someone, I mean Vina, woke me up at six in the morning, then slept the entire drive to London."

"He doesn't trust me driving." Vina shrugged.

"To be fair, you have wrecked every car you've owned."

"I've owned one car." Vina rolled her eyes. She lifted Cactus up into her arms. "Hello, un-furred one, how are you doing?"

"We brought you breakfast." Nish scratched Cactus on the head when Vina held him out towards her brother. "Want to come and check out our Airbnb with us?"

"Sure. Why not?" Motts ducked upstairs to shove a stack of photos into her backpack and a few things for Cactus. He'd enjoy being in a new space for a while. She returned to find Vina and Nish smiling a little wildly at her mother. "Something I missed?"

"You're going out?" Her mother was scowling at the twins, who seemed remarkably unbothered. She glanced between the three friends with narrowed eyes.

"You wanted me to socialise more." Motts grabbed her coat off the stand by the door. "Bye."

The twins followed her out of the house quickly. They made a rapid escape, flying down the road as if her mother might catch up to them somehow. Motts laughed when Vina grabbed a white box and handed it to her.

"What've we got?" Motts lifted the lid to find a selection of doughnuts and a few pastries. She picked up what looked like a roll of some sort. "What's this?"

"Bombay potato roll. Divine. Might have to come up with our own version at some point." Vina twisted around in the front seat so she could point out the various treats. "Pork and Fennel sausage roll. A salted caramel honeycomb doughnut. A lemon curd brûlée doughnut, especially for you. You're welcome."

"Lemon curd?" Motts abandoned the savoury treats and grabbed the doughnut. "Ah, heaven in fried form. You do love me."

"There are also a few cinnamon orange morning buns." Vina continued describing all the treasures in the box. "We wanted to balance out all the healthy food."

"Don't care." Motts took a massive bite of the doughnut. "Mum bought sugar-free lemon curd."

"Okay, but why? Does she hate joy?" Vina reached out to pat Motts gently on the hand. "We've a thermos of coffee as well. Is your mum still on her herbal tea kick?"

"Dad sneaks coffee in every morning." Motts had been impressed. It wasn't like her father to put up any kind of a fuss. "I suppose he draws the line at messing with his caffeine."

"Maybe he should draw the line at her making your life miserable," Vina muttered under her breath.

"I heard you. Nish heard you. Cactus heard you. I don't know why you're whispering when we're in a car." Motts finished off her lemon curd with a satisfied sigh. "I don't want to chat about Mum. How long are you here for?"

"Until after Christmas, when we're driving you back where you belong." Vina grabbed one of the rolls from the box that rested in Motts's lap. "River's coming up with his parents, and your grandparents might come as well the day after."

"Really?" Motts was surprised.

"Did you genuinely think we'd leave you to wither away for two weeks all by yourself?"

"Not technically by myself, was I?" Motts pointed to Cactus, who was prowling around in his little carrier. "Dempsey identified Jonty and Hugo."

"Did he?"

After nodding, Motts settled into the seat for the rest of the ride. She needed a moment of not talking. Vina observed her for a second, then twisted back around; she played with her phone, and then the latest true-crime podcast from Oz & D came from the car stereo.

Perfect.

A distraction.

I wonder if I can meet up with Osian and Dannel while I'm in London. They did respond to my email, after all. Maybe they can help with Jenny's cold case.

The Airbnb ended up being about twenty minutes from her parents' place, though traffic and a last-minute stop at Sainsbury's for a few critical supplies gave Motts plenty of time to listen to the podcast. It helped her relax. And release some of the stress from constantly dealing with her mother.

After helping carry all the groceries and luggage into the house they'd rented, Motts inspected what Vina considered critical supplies. *Beer? Crisps? And six advent calendars?* She glanced over to find Nish freeing Cactus from his carrier.

"Aren't you a bit late for advent calendars? It's the twenty-first." Motts grabbed the Maltesers one. "Claiming this one."

"See? It's never too late." Vina grinned. "They were on sale. Cheaper than buying bags of the individual treats themselves."

"More work, though." Motts poked a finger into the first door on her calendar. She popped a

Malteser into her mouth, then went to retrieve a box from her backpack. "I have photos."

"Photos? Baby Motts photos?" Vina lifted the lid off, then grabbed the one on top. "Aw. Weren't you adorable?"

"Did your parents ever think about trading her in for another model?" Motts pulled the box away from Vina.

"No one wanted her." Nish feigned sadness, then dodged out of the way of his sister's elbow. "What are we doing with all of these?"

"Looking for a serial killer." Motts headed into the living room by the electric fireplace.

"Want to warm yourself by the fire, Cactus?" Vina fiddled around with the controls before finally getting it going. "Here we are. Nish, toss me the blanket for him."

"He's so spoilt." Motts laughed.

"Don't insult my godson, Mottsy." Vina fluffed up the blanket and set Cactus in the centre of it.

Lying on the floor by the fireplace, Motts flipped through the photos. Most had come from a sports day at her school the year Jenny had been murdered. Her father had gathered them up for her.

She handed a stack to Nish and a second to Vina. "I want to separate them into two piles. One with adults and boys, and a second that just features the girls. I'm hoping we'll find Jonty, Hugo, or their parents somewhere in this stack. Sports day was the best chance I could think of for having photos of them. Dad managed to find them for me."

"How about we stroll down memory lane while finishing up the podcast?" Nish pulled YouTube up on the television and found Oz & D's channel. He held up the first photo in his stack. "I don't think I've ever seen you wear a dress like this."

Motts grimaced at the lace-covered floral monstrosity. "Mum's idea of feminine beauty. Not mine. Works for some people. Not me."

"Poor Mottsy." Vina plucked at the sleeve of Motts's knitted burnt orange cardigan. "This is much more your style."

"Who's this?" Nish held up a photo of a stylish blonde woman in her forties. "None of my teachers were ever this beautiful or put together."

"Mrs Ceresto. She was a brilliant teacher. She let me hide in her office when class was too much for me. Loved her." Motts grabbed the photo from her. "Mum hated her. She was too *modern*."

"Think she still lives in the area? She might remember something about your class or Jonty and his family." Vina crawled across the carpet to look at the photo. "She was stunning. Wow. First crush?"

"Never really had crushes." Motts shrugged.

"Pity. She'd have been mine." Vina laughed when Motts yanked the photo away from her. "Sorry, Mottsy. Why don't I do a little sleuthing on Facebook? See if she's there. You and Nish can keep going through these. I've finished with my stack already."

Half an hour later, they'd skimmed through every photo in the box. Motts had found only two with Jonty. None with his brother or family. Her parents had mostly been focused on her, after all.

And Motts had always been uncomfortable around the brothers.

"Found her." Vina thrust her phone into Motts's face, so close that her eyes crossed while trying to focus on the screen. "She's not far from here. We should go say hello. Maybe she remembers Jonty and Hugo. You said parents complained about Hugo making comments to the girls."

"Now? Right now? Immediately?" Motts leaned away from her slightly manic friend. Her plans had changed multiple times in the last twenty-four hours. It was disorienting. She didn't like it. *What if Mrs Ceresto knows something that helps solve Jenny's murder? I can do this.* "Fine. Fine. Not sure Cactus will appreciate a second ride in his carrier."

"Why don't I stay here? River's going to be driving up today. You and Vina can track down your old teacher."

"Starting off my day with potential death at the hands of her driving? Not on my holiday wish list." Motts got slowly to her feet. She gave Cactus a quick cuddle, then returned him to the blanket nest by the fire. "Let's go before I lose my nerve."

Mrs Ceresto lived on a quaint street of old houses. She'd probably lived there since before she was a teacher. It was a sweet little area. Cosy. Motts wondered if growing up here would've been a less loud experience.

"There it is." Vina had parked further up the lane. "Shall we? Ready for a trip down memory lane?"

"Not particularly." Motts climbed out of the car and leaned against it. She took a few deep breaths and steadied herself. "What if she doesn't remember me?"

"You stand out, Mottsy. In a sea of boring, you stand out." Vina winked at her. She caught Motts by the hand. "Nothing to see but ex-girlfriends on a stroll together."

"Why do I put up with you?"

They made their way down the pavement toward Mrs Ceresto's house. They had to separate when a bald man with a scruffy beard barrelled between them. Motts stumbled into the road, narrowly missing falling into a parked car.

"Oi. Wanker." Vina rushed over to help Motts to her feet. "He was in a hurry."

"Did he come from Mrs Ceresto's house?"

"In the general direction. We should hurry." Vina picked up the pace. They quickly arrived at her old teacher's house. "Do you smell something?"

Before Motts could respond, something in the distance caught her attention. She strode forward past the house. A lone figure stood at the end of the street, half hidden by a lorry.

Motts eased her phone out of her pocket, trying to get a photo that might allow her to zoom in on the hooded figure's face. "Don't move. Don't move."

"Motts?"

She dropped her phone when Vina shouted from behind her. Unfortunately, the figure had vanished by the time she retrieved it. "Bugger."

"Motts. *Motts.*"

"What?" Motts jogged back to where her friend stood banging on the door. "What's the matter?"

"I smell smoke." Vina knocked again, then

jammed the doorbell several times. *"Bugger.* Call 999. I'm going to see if I can get around back. Motts? Motts."

The smell hit Motts a second after Vina mentioned smoke. Everything around her seemed to slow down and speed up at the same time. She couldn't move; it felt like being buried under memories of the burning brewery.

"Mottsy? I'm going to call the police. Can you move back away from the house?" Vina seemed to grasp something was wrong. She caught Motts by the arm and led her a safe distance while also calling the emergency services.

"Mrs Ceresto. We should try to get into the house. Was the door unlocked?" Motts shook herself out of the memories. She checked the doorknob and found it open. "Come on, Vina."

The smoke was so thick. Motts couldn't see anything. She had no idea where Mrs Ceresto might be, if she was even in the house at all.

Shouting her teacher's name, Motts managed to get into the living room. The fire had obviously been set elsewhere in the house. The room was filled with smoke; she could hear the familiar crackling sound that threatened to drag her back into her memories.

Not now.

Breathe.

No, don't breathe; smoke is bad.

"Motts? The 999 man is telling us to stay outside. It's not safe." Vina caught her by the arm and forced her out of the house. "The firefighters are a few minutes away. I can already hear the sirens."

"We could save her." Motts wasn't sure she believed herself. She couldn't shake the image of the man she'd seen at the end of the street. Why had he been watching the house? "We have to get inside."

"Motts." Vina grabbed her by the shoulders. "Why don't you text Dempsey? This can't be a coincidence."

Nothing is a coincidence.

"We shouldn't be paranoid. Mrs Ceresto might've left something on the stove." Motts sat on the kerb, trying not to cough. The acrid smoke reminded her far too much of her brief encounter with almost being burnt to death. "I'm texting Dempsey."

Motts: My former teacher's house is on fire.

Dempsey: Pardon?

Motts: We came to ask her about Jonty and Hugo. She still lives in the village. I saw a man in a hoodie at the end of her street

then we smelt smoke. I couldn't get into the house to save her.

Dempsey: Stay out of the house. What's the address? If it's connected, I'll want the firefighters to preserve as much evidence as possible.

CHAPTER FOUR

"I could've saved her. I should've done something. Floor. You're supposed to drop to the floor to avoid the toxic air. How did I forget? Floor flailing fire." Motts fought tears while trying to pull herself together enough to finish her statement to the police, who had shown up not long after the firefighters. "There was so much smoke. We couldn't see."

"Ms Mottley? Nothing you did would've helped her. We've reason to believe she passed away before the fire started." Constable Webb was trying to be reassuring. "Was Mrs Ceresto expecting you? How did you know her?"

"She was my old teacher. I haven't been to visit in

a while, but I came to see my parents for the holidays. I...." Motts trailed off. She couldn't tell the constable she'd wanted to grill the poor woman about a potential serial killer. "I thought it might be nice to reconnect."

With her dead body.

Grim.

Why can I still smell smoke?

Jump.

"Ms Mottley?"

"Sorry?" Motts blinked a few times, realising she'd been staring at the house in silence for several minutes. "I didn't hear your question."

"Are you all right?"

"Constable? Mottsy had a near miss with a fire a few weeks ago. I imagine this brought back quite traumatic memories of having to leap from a window." Vina stepped up beside her. She wrapped an arm around Motts. "Could we have a minute to step across the street? Maybe get some fresh air?"

"We have your contact information. I'm sure the detectives will be in touch if they have any questions." Constable Webb motioned for them to go on. She turned and headed toward the house.

"C'mon, Mottsy. Why don't we sit on the kerb

across the street, yeah? Wait for your knight in detective armour to show up." Vina kept her arm around Motts. "I've messaged Nish. He's told your dad that you're going to spend the night with us. He's going to run over to pick up some clothes for you and more supplies for Cactus."

"Vina."

"No way am I leaving you to your mum's *tender* care after this." Vina sat beside her on the kerb. She nudged Motts gently with her elbow. "Want to hear some juicy gossip?"

"*Vina.*"

"Taking that as a yes. It seems your Mrs Ceresto drowned in her tub," Vina whispered. She kept sneaking glances to make sure the police were too far away to hear. "I overheard the medical examiner chatting with one of the detectives."

"How does one drown in a house fire?" Motts remembered what the constable had told her. "The police think she died before it started."

"Exactly. Maybe it was an accident?"

"Her corpse accidentally set the house on fire?" Motts closed her eyes and tried to stop thinking about flames and smoke. "Can we talk about something else for a second? Or not chat at all?"

"How about we chat about the devilishly handsome detective heading our way?" Vina teased.

Motts found herself inordinately relieved to see him striding towards them. Dempsey came straight over to them. She managed to smile wanly up at him. "Hello."

"Hello." Dempsey crouched in front of them. He held out a pair of headphones to her. "Thought you might appreciate a little dulling of the chaotic orchestra of a crime scene."

"So, not an accidental drowning?" Motts asked. She held the noise-cancelling headphones loosely in her hand. "She was murdered?"

"Undetermined. Either way, it's likely the fire wasn't the cause of her death. You were never going to be able to save her." Dempsey tapped a finger against her hand. "Why don't I have a chat with my fellow detectives? See what else I can find out."

"There was a broken picture frame by the door. I noticed it when we ran out. The glass crunched under my shoes." Motts eased the headphones onto her head. "We'll be here. Not breathing smoke."

Sitting on the kerb, Motts watched the firefighters slowly putting away their equipment. The medical examiner had taken away the body. She'd been unable to turn away despite Vina trying to distract her.

Her phone buzzed in her pocket. Probably her parents. Motts ignored it as well. There was too much happening.

Too much going on.

The fire had brought a host of bad memories. Motts hoped the nightmares weren't going to come back as well. She'd only just stopped having them.

Poor Mrs Ceresto.

Could it have been an accident?

Anything's possible.

Possible. But not plausible.

A serial killer had already hunted down almost her entire class, and then one of her former teachers had been found deceased. Dead in her tub and her house on fire? *That's one hell of an accident.*

One hell of a coincidence.

It was a while before Dempsey returned. Motts was beginning to regret not having more than doughnuts for breakfast. She couldn't tell if her stomach was rolling because of hunger or nerves. Maybe both.

"Motts? We've got to go. I've got to get ready for my date with Taara." Vina had stayed glued to her side. "She's coming in for the holidays as well."

Taara Khatri had been dating Vina for a while. She frequently travelled for her family's import/export business. She was lovely and had a massively calming influence on the occasionally chaotic Vina.

What Motts wanted to say was "okay." But she couldn't get the word out. Her gaze kept going to the fire trucks.

The smell of smoke refused to leave her. She could feel the ghostly fingers of warmth flickering across her skin. The cracking timbers. The feeling of being trapped with no escape.

Breathe.

In, one two three four five.

Out, one two three four five.

In, one two three four five.

Out, one two three four five.

Battling the memories, Motts didn't initially notice Dempsey take a seat beside her. Then, she felt a coat drop around her shoulders. *Am I shivering?*

I'm shivering. I should stop. Why can't I stop?

Why am I shaking?

Shaking shivering silliness.

Shut up.

"What shade of blue would you say the sky is today?" Dempsey asked after settling his coat around her. "Did you know Olympic blue is an actual colour?"

"Is it?" Motts managed.

"One of my detectives has all the shades of blue memorised." Dempsey stretched his long legs out in front of him. "Pigeon blue is a thing. Pigeon. Always felt they were more grey than anything else."

"This is the most absurd conversation I've ever had." Motts managed to breathe freely for the first time in minutes. "And I've had fairly odd chats with my cat."

"Possibly. Helped get you out of your flashback, though, didn't it?" He smiled. "You'll be pleased to know the police have finished up. They've agreed to allow my team to handle the potential homicide investigation because it might be related."

"DCI Byrne? Would you mind terribly giving Motts a lift? I'm running late." Vina gave Motts a mischievous grin before bolting toward her car.

"Has she always been so subtle?"

"That was for my benefit. Trying to make me laugh." Motts tugged his coat further around her. "I kept replaying jumping out of the window at the brewery. Breaking it. Wondering if I would survive."

"But you did," Dempsey reminded her. "Have you had lunch?"

"Barely had brekkie."

"Why don't I take you somewhere? We can pick up food, then go to my office. I want your impressions on Mrs Ceresto." Dempsey had his phone out. He checked his messages for several minutes before turning back to her. "You ready to get up? Or do you need a few more minutes?"

"I'm okay." Motts stood up and offered him his coat. She pointed down the street to the parked lorry. "I saw a man in a hoodie hiding there. He disappeared before I could get a photo or anything. He was watching the house."

"Watching the house or you?"

"Both?" Motts didn't know for sure. He had to have been watching the house first, though. She'd arrived to find him already there. "I couldn't see his face."

They walked down the street, avoiding the lingering emergency services personnel. Dempsey paused to speak with a couple of detective inspectors who'd just arrived. Motts figured they must be part of his cold case team.

Shoving her hands in the pockets of her cardigan, Motts kept walking toward his vehicle. She recognised it further down the street. She simply wasn't up to dealing with more strangers.

Small talk.

Saying hellos and introductions.

The day had been a lot already. She wanted to get warm. Cuddles with Cactus.

Motts heard the doors click when she arrived at the Range Rover. She climbed into the passenger side and closed her eyes. "I hope you didn't suffer, Mrs Ceresto. I'm sorry the killer found you."

Sitting in Dempsey's vehicle, Motts noticed a man wandering past on the sidewalk. She frowned at his bald head. Where had she seen him?

The man headed up the walk to the house beside Mrs Ceresto's. A neighbour? Motts suddenly remembered the man ploughing between her and Vina minutes before they'd noticed the fire.

Had he started it? Was that the reason he'd been rushing away? Could her teacher have been killed by someone completely unrelated to the deaths of her classmates?

Or maybe the neighbour had started the fire but not been involved in her death?

Dempsey arrived a few seconds later. He started the engine and got the heat going immediately. "My detectives are going to canvass the neighbours to see if anyone noticed the man you saw. We're also looking for any security cameras in the area."

"They might want to start with her immediate neighbour." Motts relayed what she remembered seeing. "Not saying the man was involved. But it is suspicious."

CHAPTER FIVE

T
HE OFFICE
D
EMPSEY REFERRED TO WAS A SMALL AREA
of the Lewisham Police Station. There was an open space with several desks plus three rooms. No windows.

"For a small space, this is the exact opposite of cosy." Motts stood awkwardly in the middle of the desks. She held two of the six pizzas they'd picked up from Pizza Express. "Where is everyone?"

"On their way back from Dulwich." Dempsey motioned for her to set the boxes on a table at the back of the room. He gestured to the dry erase board set up next to it. "This one is dedicated to your cold case."

Motts left the boxes on the table and went over

to the board. She was stunned at the visual made by the rows of images of her former classmates. "I...."

"Sobering, isn't it? To see them all lined up side by side." Dempsey came up to stand beside her. "We've laid them out chronologically after separating out the few who likely did die from natural causes."

"Starting with Jenny." Motts touched a finger to the photo of her friend. "Why us? Why our class?"

"We haven't a clue. I imagine we won't until we've spoken to the killer." Dempsey perched on the edge of one of the desks. "All we have are theories."

"And?"

"Let's have some lunch in my office. We can talk about your teacher." Dempsey deftly avoided her question. He stood and went to check through the pizza boxes before grabbing the pepperoni and sausage. "Fancy a slice or two? My team will devour all of this like locusts in a field."

Staring at the photos on the board, Motts needed a few seconds to process what Dempsey said. She couldn't seem to turn away from the vision of her classmates. They were like paper dolls.

All Motts could think was "why?" Why their class? Why take such time and deliberation? Surely the killer hadn't required thirty years.

How had no one caught them?

Pacing back and forth in front of the board, Motts read the notes jotted down underneath each photo. Dates of death, ages at the time, methods of killing. From obviously suspicious to somewhat natural causes. There had been months and even years between some of them.

"Without you, I'm not sure we would've pieced this all together." Dempsey returned to sitting on the edge of one of the desks. He used his half-eaten piece of pizza to point at the board. "Whoever this is, they're clever."

"Or lucky." Motts made herself turn away from the photos. She grabbed one of the plates and dithered about, trying to pick a slice. "Maybe both? If the killer is Hugo… he had to have been a teenager when he started."

"He wouldn't be the first." Dempsey led her into his office, motioning for her to take the seat across the desk from his. "There are serial killers who started earlier than you think. It's even possible his younger brother helped him."

"But you can't prove it one way or the other."

"Not yet." Dempsey took a bite of his pizza. He was silent for a moment. "We'll stop them, Motts."

"Before or after they complete their schoolgirl

set?" Motts couldn't help asking. "They've only got, what… four of us left?"

"We're going to stop them, whether it's Hugo or Jonathan or some other person we've yet to identify." Dempsey set his plate down and wiped his fingers on a napkin. "No one else is going to die."

"You can't promise that." Motts stared down at the previously appetising slice of pizza. She couldn't help thinking about a now elderly Mrs Ceresto, killed in her own home. "Did they figure out what happened to the broken picture frame?"

"Her teacher of the year award. There was some sort of medallion. It's missing. The killer must've smashed the glass and stolen it." Dempsey grabbed his phone, scrolling through the images to show her a photo of the frame on the floor. "We're going over everything in the home. They may have made a mistake."

"They haven't yet."

"No one is perfect." Motts picked at the crust on her pizza. She glanced through his office window over at the board. "Of the twenty girls in my class, thirteen are dead, probably murdered, four are alive, counting myself, and three you've yet to locate."

"Yes."

"Thirteen dead. Fourteen, if Mrs Ceresto winds up being connected." Motts shook her head. "How've they gotten away with it?"

"I've no idea, but I can tell you I've no intentions of allowing them to add you to the list." Dempsey spoke firmly and confidently.

It didn't make her feel better.

Well.

It made her feel slightly better.

"Shouldn't the police have an idea?"

"The police are doing their best." Dempsey reached across his desk to nudge her plate. "You should eat. Why were you visiting your teacher?"

"To say hello?" Motts took a bite of pizza, chewing slowly to avoid having to give more details. She was supposed to be more careful.

But she wanted answers.

"Motts?" Dempsey waited patiently. He chuckled when she took another bite instead of responding. "Well, at least you're eating."

"Byrne?" A detective poked her head into the office. "Ah. A visitor. Ms Mottley, I presume."

Motts glanced from the stranger over to Dempsey, then back. "Well, I'm not Dr Livingston."

"Nice. No one's ever as amused by the reference

as I am. DI Felicity Lam." She stepped further into the office. "The vultures have descended on the pizza. So, hope you didn't want more."

Dempsey shook his head. "I'm getting a statement from Motts."

"Are you?" Motts wasn't sure she'd offered much of anything even close to resembling a statement. "Sorry. Snarky snarls speaking."

"Four out of ten on your alliteration scale," Dempsey offered. He returned his attention to DI Lam. "Did they find anything on CCTV?"

She eyed Motts momentarily before answering his question. "Still waiting on a few of the cameras. We found a neighbour who saw the man in a hoodie at the end of the lane. He hopped a fence and disappeared through the small wooded area behind their house. No one got a good look at his face. Definitely a white male, though. No other identifying information. Relatively tall.

"Could be either Jonty or Hugo," Motts interjected into the conversation. "They were tall. I remember Jonty was teased for being taller than everyone in his class. Kids can be complete berks."

"They can." Dempsey tapped his finger against the desk. "Are we any closer to finding either of the brothers?"

"They're like ghosts."

"Ghosts making ghosts," Motts muttered. She tried to scrunch down into the chair when both detectives glanced in her direction. "Ghosts don't exist."

Grabbing her backpack off the floor, Motts retrieved the set of noise-cancelling headphones that Dempsey had lent to her. She shoved them on and tried to breathe through the sudden rush of anxiety. *You are fine.*

Fine.

Safe, perfectly safe in a building filled with police officers.

Safely shadowing... I need a different alliteration word.

With her eyes closed, Motts continued to count her breaths. It helped. And then, it didn't.

The silence helped more.

She lost track of time while repeating numbers in her head. Counting her breathing worked so much better when she had Cactus with her. She managed eventually to return to some semblance of normalcy.

Motts opened her eyes to find herself alone in Dempsey's office. Lights turned off. He'd stepped out to offer her privacy and taken his detective with him. "Okay. Time to get it together."

A knock sounded on the door. Motts peered over to find Dempsey outside his own office. She waved him inside, feeling a little embarrassed.

"Don't apologise." He interrupted before she could even start. "You've had a dreadful day. An overwhelming one. You're entitled to want a quiet space to yourself for a while."

"But it's your office…."

"It appears unharmed."

"You've really got to stop inhaling literature. It bleeds out of your pores." Motts poked a finger at her now cold pizza. "Did you have other questions?"

"You didn't answer the one I asked, but I imagine they can all wait." Dempsey returned to his seat.

"Can they?" She hated having wasted his time. Surely he had better things to do than wait for her to put herself back together. "I've been going through old photos. My dad found them for me from some sports day at school."

"Oh?"

"I hoped maybe we'd catch a glimpse of both brothers. We didn't, just the one with Jonty. There was a photo of my old teacher." Motts fished around in her backpack to find it and placed it on his desk. "We figured maybe she'd remember something that I didn't."

"Adults often do."

Motts nodded immediately. "Exactly. My perspective on my classmates, on Jonty and Hugo, is all from when I was so much younger. Kids see things differently. Me more than most, I think."

"We're trying to get a lead on any other teachers. Your thinking was right in line with mine. Sadly, many have already passed away. All from natural causes, thankfully," Dempsey rushed to clarify when she frowned in concern. "We're also going through Mrs Ceresto's files. She kept all of them. We're hoping she mentioned the Barbrows."

With a bit of encouragement from Dempsey, Motts walked him through the brief encounter with the dodgy neighbour. She gave him the details of the house and fire. What she could remember, at least.

"I froze."

"A perfectly natural response when confronted with an event triggering post-traumatic stress." Dempsey stood from his chair and came around his desk to sit on the edge of it in front of her. "Nothing you did could've saved Mrs Ceresto. Nothing. She was dead hours before the fire started. Hours, Motts. Nothing you did would've made a difference. It's not on you."

"It feels like it is."

"Feelings, on occasion, lie. Particularly when connected to past trauma." Dempsey lightly kicked her foot with his. "How about I take you back to your friends? Cactus must be missing you by now."

CHAPTER SIX

"Mottsy!" Vina greeted her enthusiastically when she opened the door to their Airbnb. She dropped her arms. "Quiet evening?"

Motts nodded. She lifted Cactus into her arms when he rubbed against her leg. He butted his head against her chin. "Did you have a good day?"

Meow.

"I'll text you with any changes in the case. Try to relax." Dempsey gave Cactus a quick touch on the head. "Take care of her."

Heading into the house, Motts sat on the chair closest to the fire. It was a rainy late December afternoon. The chill had settled into her bones.

A blanket appeared in front of her. Motts tilted her head back to find Nish holding the soft fleece over her. She accepted with a grateful smile and dragged it around her body; Cactus immediately leapt up into her lap and curled up on top of the soft fabric.

"Spoilt little monster." Nish laughed.

The twins gave her space for a while. Vina put a video on the telly for her. A playlist of one of their favourite channels. It allowed Motts to relax even further, some of the stress from the morning fading away.

It was over an hour before the quiet chaos in her mind settled down. She no longer felt as though someone had shoved cotton into her ears. And it didn't take tremendous effort to put a fully formed thought together.

"When's River getting here?" Motts made it through several videos before she was ready to speak. "I thought he'd already have arrived by now."

"His parents decided to drive with him." Nish handed a mug of tea to her. He stretched out on the couch and grunted when Vina flopped onto him. "Oi. I am not a cushion."

"Auntie Lily and Uncle Tomato are driving with him? They'll literally stop at every single shop she finds interesting from Looe to London." Motts couldn't help snickering at her poor cousin's misfortune. "He'll whinge for days about this."

"One of these days, you're going to have to explain the Uncle Tomato thing." Vina got off her brother and returned to the kitchen. "Anyone want snacks?"

"I can't explain. I don't remember why I started calling him Uncle Tomato." Motts shrugged. She grabbed the bag of Monster Munch Roast Beef crisps when Vina offered one to her. "Dempsey said Mrs Ceresto died before the fire was set."

"Did he?" Vina came over to sit on the arm of the chair, sinking in until she was squashed against Motts. "Any other information you gleaned from our silver fox?"

"Do you mind?" Motts pressed Cactus into Vina's arms and got to her feet. She retrieved her backpack, then went to sit by the coffee table. "I have a few projects to finish up."

"You're supposed to be on holiday." Nish watched her pull out her quilling supplies. "What are you working on?"

"A series of Christmas pudding ornaments. I found the perfect metal rings that work as a frame to place the rolled papers inside." Motts opened the box and carefully retrieved one of her finished examples. "Aren't they sweet?"

The ornaments were relatively small, a circle filled with scrolls of brown paper on the bottom to represent the pudding, then white on top. She'd glued red berries and green leaves that were all made out of quilled paper to represent holly, with a little bit of thread at the top.

"These are brilliant." Vina gently plucked another one from the box. "You're so talented. How do you do this with paper?"

"Carefully," Motts teased.

They were going to be gifts for her friends and family. Most everyone would be in London for the holidays for a change. She still had about ten left to make. It wouldn't take a massive amount of time to finish.

November had been spent working on a lot of quilling projects. Motts had intentionally planned to shut her paper bouquet shop down for several weeks in December. However, it had worked out when she wound up having to go to London.

She had one final project outside of the ornaments. It was a long-term project. She was making a Sherlock Holmes for Osian and Dannel from the Oz and D podcast. Osian's younger sister had emailed

Motts several weeks earlier, asking if she could make the quilling project. It had been last minute, but she'd agreed.

A paper version of the infamous profile of the detective with his hat, pipe, and magnifying glass. It was a large project. Motts had left it at her parents' house. She had a few more lines left to work on it, then she'd be meeting with the couple to surprise them.

A present to herself, really. Motts had wanted to meet them for a while now, since she listened to their podcast religiously. Dannel was the first fellow autistic she'd known to be as interested in true crime as she was.

River, Nish, and Vina planned to go with her. They were all fans of the podcast. Motts wanted to share details of her cold case with the pair as well.

They might think of something Motts hadn't.

That the police hadn't.

"River texted. They're an hour away. It's only taken them four extra hours." Nish waved his phone, then returned to messaging with his boyfriend. "He should be glad his parents decided to rent their own place for the holidays—even if it is just down the street."

"Your mum has been calling me every twenty

minutes, by the way." Vina held her phone up when it began to ring again.

"Do you really have the *Jaws* theme tune as the ring tone for my mum?" Motts wasn't sure she should be laughing. But she couldn't stop herself from snickering. "Since when?"

"Seemed the appropriate level of warning so I don't accidentally answer." Vina winked at her. "Since River and Nish will be reacquainting themselves, want to watch a movie with Taara and me?"

"What you're saying is that you both have dates this evening and don't want me to feel left out?" Motts didn't see the point of dancing around what was obviously the issue. "I don't need to be entertained."

"Well…"

"I will be fine alone. Why don't you two go out?" Motts could genuinely think of nothing lovelier than having an entire house to herself after being trapped with her parents for days. "More than fine. I've got Cactus."

The twins both stared at her. Fidgeted in silence. Stared at her some more. Motts was growing as uneasy as they seemed to be.

"What?"

"Just make sure to keep the doors locked." Vina

finally spoke after a lengthy silence where the twins had simply stared at each other. "And text one of us if anything happens."

"What do you think is going to happen?" Motts rolled her eyes. "And if it does, I'm texting Dempsey, not you. You panic."

"I panicked one time," Vina grumbled.

"You called the police because I said I needed help." Motts had to laugh when Vina covered her ears and pretended not to listen. "You had Hughie rush up to my cottage only for the poor constable to discover Cactus had gotten trapped in his cardigan and I needed a spare set of hands to catch him."

"He did help."

"Not the point."

Ensconcing herself further into the armchair by the fire, Motts allowed the twins to make their date preparations. It was like watching a nature show. She found their nerves about going out with their significant others amusing.

Vina had been with Taara for months now. Nish had known River since childhood. How did they still have anxiety over going out on dates with them?

Neurotypicals were weird.

So weird.

She barely had a second to say hello to her

cousin. Instead, he dropped a container of walnut cookies in her lap. They were traditional Chinese treats that his mum had obviously made.

"Save some for us." He grinned before dragging Nish out of the house.

Save some? Peeling the lid off the container, Motts counted at least fifty cookies. How many did he think she could eat in one evening?

"What do you think?" Vina swirled into the living room in a dark blue sari with silver detailing. She'd draped it in a more modern style, giving her freedom of movement. "We're going dancing."

"Beautiful. This one of your mum's old saris?" Motts thought she'd seen a similar fabric in one of Leena's old photos from her days as an actress.

"Yes. Isn't it lovely? She let me have it tailored for myself." Vina paused in front of a mirror to adjust her hair. "Must run. I'm picking up Taara. Lock the door behind me."

Motts followed Vina to the door, making sure to double-check the locks. "You'd think I'd never been alone."

Returning to the living room, Motts sat on the floor by the coffee table. She wanted to wrap up the last of the ornaments. She intended to give all her family a collection of them.

Small, sweet presents made by her own hands.

Motts was ten paper Christmas puddings into her evening when Cactus climbed out from under the blanket on the chair behind her. She watched him prowl down the hall to sit by the front door. "Something wrong?"

Meow.

Cactus stayed by the front door, periodically meowing while Motts frowned at him. Vina and Nish had keys. No one else had plans to come over. Not even her aunt and uncle. River had said they'd gone over to see her parents.

Vina's never going to let me forget this if something goes wrong.

"Cactus?" Motts went over to grab the tablet off the kitchen table. It had access to the Ring camera. "There's no one out there."

Maybe I should call the police? Or text Dempsey, at least? See what he thinks?

Sitting at the table, Motts stared at the live video feed. Nothing stood out to her from the darkness. She kept watching until a bang against the kitchen window caused her to scream.

Bugger.

With the tablet in one hand, Motts bolted out of the kitchen. She grabbed Cactus and darted for the nearest bedroom. Locking the door, she hid inside the closet and sent a text to Dempsey.

Motts: I think someone's outside the Airbnb.

Dempsey: I'm on my way. I'm calling into the station to have the closest constables on patrol respond.

Motts: It's probably nothing. Maybe some kid threw a rock against the kitchen window as a joke.

Dempsey: Better to be overly cautious than living with regrets.

CHAPTER SEVEN

Motts sat on the floor of the closet with Cactus curled up behind her. She clutched her phone tightly, waiting for any sign of the intruder. It beeped in her hand, and she dropped it. "Holy mother of mittens."

Breathe before you give yourself a stroke and do the killer a favour and kill yourself without his help.

Hunting around for her phone, Motts eventually found it. Dempsey had texted her. He'd arrived outside, along with several other police officers.

No sign of an intruder aside from the mess of footprints in the garden. Dempsey told her to come and unlock the door for him. It took several tries before Motts was able to stand up.

Her legs were shaky. She felt like the video of a

newborn giraffe she'd seen the other day on YouTube. Cactus followed her to the front door and immediately raced over to Dempsey, who lifted him up.

Motts held tightly to the doorframe. She'd been genuinely frightened by the banging against the window. Her memory was still fresh of Mrs Ceresto dying and her house on fire. "Maybe I imagined it all."

"You didn't." Dempsey shook his head. He set Cactus down, then stepped over to her, gently taking her by the arms. "Let's get you inside. I've already spoken with the constables and my team. We'll have someone watching for the rest of the night. First, we're going to have forensics do a thorough search of the back garden and around the outside of the kitchen window."

"Inspector Byrne?" One of his detectives stepped over with something in his hand. It had been placed in an evidence bag. "We found this resting against the fence along the back of the garden. From the damage to the wood, the prowler clambered over it to get away."

Dempsey took the bag and moved into the light from the house. "Teacher of the year. Can't read the date clearly; looks like 90 something or other."

"Oh my…." Motts had no doubt whatsoever it was the missing medallion from her former teacher's house. The one from the broken frame. "How did they find me here?"

"See if we can get any prints or DNA off this." Dempsey handed the evidence bag back to his detective. He motioned for Motts to return to the house; Cactus followed them inside. "Have you or your friends been posting about the house online? On Instagram, maybe?"

"I only use social media for Hollyhock Folded Blooms, my Etsy business. I post pictures of my origami and quilling creations." Motts never allowed any of her accounts to put her exact location. "Vina might've. She's on Instagram all the time. They were going out dancing. Maybe she posted her outfit from the house first?"

Vina.

They're going to freak if I don't text them.

If I do text them, they're going to bail on their dates.

"Motts? Are you okay?"

"I've been better. Never imagined having to go into the closet." Motts tried to find the energy to smile. "They could've easily broken into the house. Why knock on the window, leave the medallion, then flee?"

"Maybe they heard someone outside. Something scared them away." Dempsey sat on the sofa. He chuckled when Cactus immediately leapt up beside him, then climbed onto his shoulder. "Did you keep her safe? Good guard kitten. I'll sneak you a treat next time I'm here."

From outside the house, Motts heard a familiar voice arguing with detectives. *Oh no.* She'd forgotten her auntie and uncle were likely to return from her parents' place early. They'd notice all the police blocking the street.

"Someone you know?"

"My uncle and auntie." Motts groaned. She rushed out of the house to find them trying to push through the constables blocking their path. "Can you tell them it's okay?"

"You can let them through, Constable Edwards." Dempsey got the attention of the two officers who were in a heated discussion with her uncle. "They're family."

Motts had to hide a smile when she noticed Cactus still perched on Dempsey's shoulders. "My cat has a serious obsession with the police."

"Hello, young Pineapple." Her uncle rushed straight over to her. He looked her up and down before holding his arms out. "Hug? To soothe my nerves."

"Your nerves? He's fine." Her auntie Lily seemed to be inspecting Dempsey more than Motts. "Good. You're here to keep her safe."

"Auntie Lily." Motts groaned before giving her uncle a hug. "Please don't tell Mum and Dad. You know what Mum is like. She'll be even more suffocating."

And insufferable.

And she'll try to lock me into my childhood bedroom for the rest of my life.

Maybe I can sneak back to Cornwall before anyone notices I've gone?

"Ms Mottley is perfectly fine. We're not sure who threw the rock at the window. Likely some local prankster." Dempsey didn't blink an eye while Motts stared at him. "We're investigating thoroughly just to be certain. I can promise you that we'll do everything possible to keep her safe."

Motts continued to stare at Dempsey while her uncle and auntie headed into the house. "Santa might put you on the naughty list for lying."

"All in the name of a good cause." He carefully lifted Cactus off his shoulder and placed him into Motts's arms. "I'm going to return to the office. I want to see if they've found anything on CCTV. One of the constables will keep watch overnight. Text me if anything happens. *Immediately.*"

"I'll be fine." *I will. I'm sure it's going to be okay. It has to be.*

"Motts." Dempsey stepped closer to her. "Promise me that you'll be as careful as you possibly can. Whoever this killer is, they have an absolute obsession with your class. As if they want a complete set of schoolgirls no matter how long it takes them to achieve their goal. You are on the list. Don't take unnecessary risks. Please."

"I don't even take necessary ones when I can avoid them." Motts was always risk-averse in general. "I'll do my best."

"Good enough for me." He reached out to squeeze her shoulder. "Do you have any plans tomorrow?"

"I get to meet Oz and D. From the podcast." Motts managed a genuine grin. She was quite excited.

"Osian Garey?"

"You know them?" Motts set Cactus down when he wiggled in her arms. He immediately headed into the house, probably in search of her uncle and auntie, who doted on him. "Do you listen to their podcast?"

"Garey and I are part of a therapy group for people who work in all the branches of the emergency services. It was created to help those with post-traumatic stress." Dempsey canted his head to the side while observing her. "You might chat about your experience with the fire to them. They'd both understand what you went through."

"Maybe." Motts shrugged. "I should head inside. Don't want to leave my auntie and uncle with too long to think about what happened. Not sure they're going to believe so many police showed up for a prank."

"Text me, all right? If you need anything." He waited until she stepped back toward the house to head over to speak with the constable parked across the road.

Returning to the house, Motts pulled her phone out of her pocket. She sent a quick message to their group chat. Vina, Nish, and River didn't need to return and be shocked by the police presence.

They'd be more upset than they already would be. Motts kept things simple, though. They didn't need all the terrifying details. *Is having someone bang on your window all that scary?*

Probably if you consider who the someone is.

Not helping.

Not helping thinking about how many deaths they're responsible for.

I'll tell them it's a prank for the moment.

"Are you all right, young Pineapple?" Her uncle stood waiting for her by the door. "It wasn't some local hooligan, was it?"

"Uncle Tomato." She didn't want to worry anyone in her family unnecessarily.

"The police don't leave someone sitting outside your house for a prank." He gestured toward where the constable was parked. "Is it Jenny's killer then?"

"They don't know for sure." *Not a lie.*

Also, not entirely the truth.

CHAPTER EIGHT

"ARE YOU AWAKE?"

Motts was not surprised to wake up to Vina sitting on the end of her bed. She'd gone to bed before any of them had returned from their dates, hoping to avoid confrontation or questions, possibly both. "Yes, I am somehow managing to sleep through you poking my toe and repeatedly asking if I'm awake yet. Poking pokes poked pokily."

"Is pokily a word?"

"It is now. Not sure it's the right word, but it is one." Motts sat up and shoved her pillow behind her to lean against. She smiled when Cactus trundled across the blankets into her lap. "Why are you poking me?"

Vina grabbed her phone and practically pressed it into Motts's face. "Do you see this?"

"Not really. You've shoved the screen so close my eyes have gone all funny." Motts reared her head back a little. "Nope, still can't read it."

"Our group chat."

"Ah, yes." Motts had known the inquisition was coming. "Aren't we supposed to be driving into Covent Garden today?"

"We've time for breakfast and questions." Vina stretched out across the end of the bed. "Well?"

"Why don't we talk over breakfast? River and Nish will want to hear this as well." Motts didn't want to repeat herself over and over. She was definitely going to require caffeine and toast for the conversation as well. "Can I shower in peace, or are you going to sit outside the door?"

"Fine, fine." Vina grabbed Cactus and headed out of the room. "I'll take him on a leisurely stroll in the garden so you don't have an excuse to put us off."

"Just don't forget his sweater."

"Would I forget to clothe my beloved godson?"

Motts could hear Vina's laughter through the closed door. "Honestly."

Why do I put up with them?

Rushing through her usual morning routine, Motts finished up in the shower. She paused in front of the mirror over the sink. So much had happened in the past week that she hadn't had time to be nervous about meeting Osian and Dannel.

Until now.

Hello, I'm Motts. I listen to your podcast.

Great, I sound like I'm going door-to-door attempting to sell them a Hoover.

Hi. I'm Motts.

They know I'm Motts.

"Knock, knock." Vina interrupted her conversation practice session. "Quit planning what to say and come have some toast before it gets all moist and disgusting or the boys eat all of it."

"There are three loaves in the kitchen."

"Moist. *Moist.*"

Motts cracked the door open enough to glare at her ex-girlfriend. "Go away so I can get dressed. I can make fresh toast."

With the room to herself again, Motts grabbed a clean pair of jeans, her comfiest T-shirt, and a cardigan. She wanted to make things easier. Comfortable clothes meant one less potential sensory trigger.

She placed her noise-cancelling headphones in

her backpack. They might come in handy if things in London got too loud for her. Cactus would be going back to her parents' house since she didn't want to leave the poor dear alone all day.

It would also give her mum a chance to see she hadn't died overnight.

They were going to leave out the potential intruder.

The toast was not damp. And not eaten. It was still in the breadbox.

Motts stepped into the kitchen to find coffee and a quiche from a local café. It was one her dad went to all the time. "What's this?"

"Breakfast."

Motts sniffed at the quiche when Nish slid the plate over to her. "Where's the toast?"

"Constable outside claims a certain DCI dropped off the coffee and quiche. It was massive. The quiche." River was half asleep, slouched in a chair at the kitchen table. "Have you heard anything about the prank?"

"Well…." Motts took a bite of quiche, giving herself time to think.

"Well?" River prompted impatiently. "My dad texted me. Worried. You don't worry about some little twit running around banging on windows."

"Well," Motts repeated. She picked at the little tomatoes sunken into the quiche. "Whoever banged on the window left a present. The stolen 'Teacher of the Year' medallion from Mrs Ceresto's house."

"So not a local hooligan." Vina clutched her mug of coffee tightly. "I knew it. I knew it. You went quiet so quickly last night. Who goes to bed so early? You're always up playing with paper."

"I didn't want to worry everyone. You were on dates."

"Sod our dates, Mottsy," Vina grumbled.

"What could you have done? Hmm? The police were already here. Whoever left the medallion was gone before they arrived. They never attempted to get into the house." Motts forced herself to take another bite of quiche. She wasn't going to be put off a delicious breakfast. "They, if it was Hugo or Jonty, didn't do anything aside from stomping all over the garden, knocking on the window, and scaring the life out of me."

"Well, let's make sure they don't take the life out of you." Nish gave her shoulder a little squeeze before moving over to sit next to River at the table. "I imagine you didn't want everyone hovering over you last night. So I more than understand why you waited to tell us."

Vina glowered petulantly at her twin brother. He rolled his eyes in response. "Yes, yes, we understand."

"Wonderful. Can I finish my quiche without the guilt-induced heartburn?" Motts glanced at the clock on the wall near the fridge. She'd slept longer than she anticipated. "We're going to be late if we don't hurry. Traffic's going to be a nightmare this time of day—and year."

"It's London. Traffic is always a nightmare. No matter where you are," Nish pointed out helpfully. He ignored the grumbling sent in his direction. "What? I'm not responsible for the roadways."

"Why are we driving into Covent Garden three days before Christmas?" River whined. "Couldn't they have come to Dulwich instead?"

"And miss Covent Garden at Christmas? Not likely. Besides, we're not driving the entire way. We'll park and take the train." Motts had already carefully planned out their journey. She finished her quiche while her friends argued about the easiest way to travel.

Getting her friends out of the rented house into Vina's car required almost as much energy as wrangling a herd of cats. Motts had never tried to gather up a mass of kittens. She imagined it would still be more straightforward than cajoling three grown adults.

"I could go by myself." Motts had finally gotten tired of trying to get them out of the house. "I bet Dempsey would go with me."

"Nope. We're ready." Vina popped back into the living room with her bag, looking fashionably warm. "Taara's meeting us at the Covent Garden station."

"Wonderful. If we ever actually make it."

Dropping off Cactus with her parents turned out far simpler than getting everyone into the car had been. Her mum had gone out shopping. Her dad gave her a quick hug, then disappeared into the house with Cactus close on his heels.

They drove most of the way into the city, parking at an underground station and riding the rest of the way to Covent Garden. It was easier than trying to find somewhere closer. Not this time of year. People were enjoying the last few days leading up to Christmas.

There was a festival. Shopping. A lot of people in the area. Motts wondered if maybe they should've met in Dulwich instead.

Fewer people.

Less chaos.

"You okay, Mottsy?" Vina stayed by her side while they exited the train at Covent Garden. "Are we taking the lift or struggling up the steps?"

"Steps." Motts refused to get into a lift if at all possible. She had nightmares about being in one when it plummeted. "You can get in the small box of death."

Box of death.

Halfway up the hundred-something steps leading out of the station, Motts almost regretted her lift phobia. It would at least be easier on the way back to Dulwich.

The station was crowded. Motts felt the crush of trying to move up the stairs with loads of people going in both directions. Finally, she reached the top step, pausing when a man darted in front of her.

She caught a flash of blue eyes. Pale. Hidden in the shadows of his hoodie. She had a brief glance at his face, then everything seemed to go too fast for her to focus.

I know you.

Why do I know you?

"Pardon—" Motts never got to finish her statement. He slammed his hand against her, shoving her backwards into a stranger.

For a brief second, Motts thought she'd been

stopped from falling. Instead, the momentum from her shove sent her flying down the first flight of steps. Hands tried to catch her—and failed.

She heard Vina's scream, then her head hit a step with a painful thud.

CHAPTER NINE

MOTTS WOKE TO THE SOUNDS OF BEEPING MACHINES and the awful smell of hospital sanitiser. "Merry sodding Christmas to me."

Opening her eyes, Motts realised she was indeed in a hospital room of some sort. Her head hurt. She noticed a slightly familiar man sitting next to her bed.

"Hello. Fancy meeting you here." He grinned. "I'm the Oz half of Oz and D. I'm usually the one waking up in this hospital. It's almost nice to be on this side of things for once. Except you've gotten hurt."

"Hello." Motts grimaced at the bright light in the room. She lightly touched her head and winced when she hit a sensitive spot. "What happened?"

"You were pushed down some stairs. Your

friends are being questioned by the police." Osian raised his hand when she started to stand up. "Not like that. I just mean they're giving their statements. Your friend DCI Byrne is coordinating with my friend, Haider Khan. What do you remember?"

"Falling." Motts closed her eyes and tried to bring back the memory. "I saw someone. I think. A man."

"Interesting. Let me see if any of your friends are back. They've been worried." Osian got to his feet. He gave a little wave. "It's lovely to finally meet you. Dannel's at home. He had a stressful morning. All the people. We thought, perhaps, we might visit you in Dulwich instead. We can chat on the way. The detectives are going to give you all a ride. I'm going to step out, let DCI Byrne know you're awake."

Motts managed to nod. She rested her head against the pillow, thankful to have managed to raise the bed into a position that allowed her to sit up. "Mum's definitely going to hear about this."

Alone in the room, Motts discovered that aside from her head, nothing else seemed to hurt. She thought there might be a bruise developing on her arm. Not much else. *Where are my things?*

Dempsey walked into the room while she tried to find her bag. "Missing something?"

"My bag."

"Your cousin has it at the moment." He came over to the bed and peered down at her. "I've never driven across London quite so quickly in my entire career. How's the head?"

"Still attached." Motts shrugged, then winced when her headache throbbed at the movement. "I saw him."

"Who?"

"The man who shoved me." Motts struggled with faces at times, remembering them. She knew she'd seen him somewhere. "Do you have any photos of Jonty or Hugo? I think it might've been one or the other."

"I'll get one of my detectives to text me photos. First, let's make sure you're not suffering any lingering issues." Dempsey reached his hand out towards her, then seemed to rethink and pulled it back to his side. "You've a mild concussion. The doctor isn't keeping you for observation. They'll likely recommend someone keep an eye on you for the next twenty-four hours. You were fortunate. The crowd at the station likely saved your life. They didn't completely stop your fall, but they kept you from going any further than you did."

"Small mercies."

"Indeed." He motioned to the side of her bed,

perching on the edge of the mattress when she nodded. "What do you remember?"

"Floating."

"Floating?"

"Floating flotation floors futility." Motts rubbed her forehead and tried to take a few measured breaths. "He shoved me in my upper body. I lost my footing and went backwards. It felt like floating because of the crowd of people. I slipped through the bodies and went down. I don't remember anything after hitting my head."

"You saw his face?" Dempsey asked. "Did he say anything?"

Bringing her mind back to the incident, Motts tried to recall the face of the man who'd pushed her. She couldn't. Not even one feature or his eye colour. It felt like something was holding the details just out of reach.

"He didn't say anything I can remember. But I did see his face. I can't describe him for you." Motts hated that certain things slipped from her mind no matter how hard she tried. "If you've a picture of the brothers, I can tell you if it was one of them."

"CCTV shows a person in a hoodie waiting at the top of the stairs. They moved closer when you came into view." Dempsey used his phone to show her a clip of the footage. "They knew you'd be arriving."

"How?"

Dempsey placed her phone on the bed next to her hand. "Someone hacked your phone. They've been tracking you through the GPS on it. The same person appears to have gained access to Vina's Instagram account. She posted images of Covent Garden, talking about the trip today. She didn't mention you, but I imagine it wasn't a massive stretch to assume you'd be with her."

"Tracking my phone?" Motts shoved her phone away from her.

"We've turned off the GPS tracking on it. I had someone take a look to make sure it's safe, so they shouldn't be able to hack in again." Dempsey chuckled. "It's safe to touch your phone."

Motts couldn't help staring suspiciously at it anyway. "I'll make sure Vina stops tagging her location on Instagram."

"We've already had a few words about it." Dempsey glanced back at the door when someone knocked. "I'm guessing the doctor wants to check on you. I'll go grab your family so they can visit when the doc's finished."

Hospitals were always a nightmare for Motts.

Sounds, smells, lights. Everything bombarded her senses. She wished she had her headphones. At least it would allow her to block out one of the problems.

The lovely doctor who came into her room took Motts through a series of tests. Finally, they came to the conclusion that she was not seriously injured. She had a headache and a few bruises but had otherwise come out of her tumble down the steps unscathed.

"Do you have any questions?"

Motts stared at the doctor's chin and considered the query. "How'd I manage a private room?"

"DCI Byrne believed you'd do better with a more controlled environment. Less noise, at the very least." They smiled. "You should be ready to go within the next thirty minutes or so, which I'm sure will be a relief."

It would be, so Motts simply nodded. She wasn't up to a conversation with strangers. Her head ached a little; not massively, though.

"Motts." River came into the room first with the twins close behind. They rushed over to her. "Are you all right?"

"She fell down a flight of stairs. How do you think she's doing?" Vina snarked. She was always narkier when stressed.

"I'm fine." Motts didn't think any of them really believed her. "Honestly. The doctor says I can go soon. I don't even need a follow-up appointment."

"We were right there. We couldn't do anything." River grabbed her hand tightly. He seemed to be checking her over for injuries. "We haven't told any of the parental units. Not yours, or mine, or theirs."

"They'd only panic," Nish added. "We did tell your dad that we'd been delayed in London, so you'd be home tomorrow."

"Mum's going to be…." Motts had no words for how difficult her mother was likely to be with her being gone for two days. "I can't believe my day with Osian and Dannel got ruined by a serial killer."

"Irony at its finest? You brought the crime to Oz & D's true-crime podcast." Vina gave her a worried smile. "Are you certain you're okay?"

"Promise. Mild headache. I imagine a lovely hot bath will help with the other aches and pains from bashing into people and stairs." Motts tried not to remember the sensation of falling. She hoped it wasn't going to be a new addition to her nightmares. "River? Do you have my bag?"

River reached around to grab her backpack and set it next to her. He laughed when she immediately dug around in the bag for her headphones. "Tired of the beeps and buzzes of the hospital?"

"Definitely." Motts hit the on switch for the noise-cancelling function and immediately got the blessed relief of silence. "Brilliant."

CHAPTER TEN

"Remember how I was supposed to come to London for holidays because I'd be safer?" Motts glanced over at Dempsey, who was driving them back to Dulwich. "I've found a dead body, a burning house, and been shoved down a flight of stairs."

"Our logic was flawed, in hindsight," Dempsey admitted. "At least you can spend a quiet evening with your friends with Osian and Dannel, since they've come along for the ride."

"Quiet? Have you met my friends?" Motts glanced behind her when they all disagreed with her at the same time. "Point. Proven."

"We can't all enjoy the quiet," Vina argued. "Besides, you enjoy spending time with us."

"Introverts need to recharge their social batteries." Motts adjusted the duvet around her. Dempsey had surprised her when he'd pulled out the weighted blanket and draped it over her when she'd gotten into his vehicle.

"Some days, you recharge so much you might as well be a glow-in-the-dark Mottsy," Vina retorted.

"Glow-in-the-dark Mottsy." Motts broke into giggles with Vina. "Remember Glo Worms?"

"Creepy worms with shiny arses? Vaguely recall them. Nish begged for one, then had nightmares," Vina teased her brother, who chose to ignore her.

"I dismantled mine because I wanted to understand how the light worked." Motts remembered her mother getting so upset. She'd always enjoyed taking things apart, though. It comforted her. "Weird glowing bottoms."

The rest of the trip through late afternoon traffic was spent discussing the oddest toys from their childhood. Dempsey chimed in with the Teddy Ruxpin, a talking plushie they all agreed gave them nightmares.

They finally arrived at the Airbnb. Motts allowed Vina to drag her upstairs. She opted for a quick shower instead of the long bath she wanted. They had guests.

Guests that would know she was sitting in the

bath. It illogically bothered Motts. She showered, then changed into the spare set of clothes she still had.

She'd expected to be stressed by the sheer number of people in the house. Seven was a lot. Plus Cactus, who River had retrieved from her parents'. He thoroughly enjoyed all the attention from everyone.

Motts did not.

She wound up sitting on the couch next to Dannel, both wearing noise-cancelling headphones. They were talking via text message on their phones. Sending memes back and forth. She didn't even see the chaotic conversation happening around her.

After an hour, Motts was settled enough to adjust the level of noise cancellation. Dempsey moved from the kitchen to join them. He glanced at the meme on her phone.

"Conversing in pictures? The modern-day version of cave drawings?" Dempsey grinned at her.

"Sometimes a picture is worth a thousand words. Or at least, four." Motts had to laugh when Dannel muttered about not confusing the aged under his breath. "Think I might qualify for that category. I'm certainly older than you and Osian."

"Motts? Can we take a walk?" Dempsey stood up.

Ignoring the sudden silence from her friends, Motts followed the inspector outside. He stopped to lean against his vehicle. She thought he seemed genuinely concerned.

"I'll be careful." Motts jumped into conversation when the silence became too much.

"I imagine you're always careful." Dempsey chuckled. He tossed his keys up into the air a few times. "I'm going to have one of my detectives keep an eye on your parents' place and this one. Just in case."

Motts fidgeted with the sleeve of her cardigan. "Mum will be thrilled."

"She never has to know."

"Mum always knows." Motts watched curiously when Dempsey pulled his phone out. He showed her two photos. "Jonty and Hugo?"

"The very same. The bald one is Jonty. Hugo is the older of the two, which you already know." He continued to hold his phone while she switched back and forth between the two images. "Was it either of them?"

"They could *almost* be twins. Maybe fraternal. They're so similar." Motts used her finger to scroll between the two images. "Maybe Jonty? I think. I saw him for the briefest second. It's such a blur. Are they working together?"

"I can't say for certain."

"Is that DCI speak for yes?" Motts pulled her hand away from his phone. "We'll all be careful."

"Right." Dempsey put his phone away, then continued to watch her. She fidgeted again under the intensity of his gaze. "I'll keep in touch. Update you if we happen to find anything on the troublesome brothers. Call me? If anything seems even slightly off?"

"Promise." Motts nodded.

Despite the frigid air buffeting her, Motts remained outside even after Dempsey had driven off. She spotted the detective parked across the road. It was tempting to bring him some hot chocolate or something to help pass the time.

It had to be the dullest task in the world. Stuck in an uncomfortable car, watching a house on the off chance a killer showed up. Jonty or Hugo couldn't possibly be foolish enough to show up for a second time.

"Motts?"

She glanced behind her to find Osian joining her. "Tired of my silly friends?"

"No sillier than mine." He smiled. "How's your head?"

"Still there. Both the head and the mild ache," Motts admitted. "Dempsey—DCI Byrne mentioned you met through a therapy group."

"More support than official therapy. We've all experienced stress and trauma working as cops, paramedics, or firefighters. It helps to have someone to talk through the nightmares, I've found." Osian stepped up beside her. He had his hands shoved into his pockets. "I remember your email about the last murder you helped solve. At the brewery? I imagine seeing a house fire brought back some not so brilliant memories."

"A little." Motts shifted uneasily. "The smell, mostly. The sounds. The crackling of wood. Smoke so thick you'd think you could slice it like cake. And a feeling like my feet are glued to the floor. I can't move. Jump. Do anything to save myself."

"Dannel used to come home from his shifts smelling of smoke. It permeates everything. He always said you could taste it for days after a fire." Osian searched in his pockets, then pulled out a card. "We have an online group. Our own Discord server. We talk about nothing and everything. Sometimes it's just memes and jokes. You should join. It's for people like us. Survivors. Nice to not have to explain the flashbacks and nightmares. You'd be welcome."

"I've never worked in any facet of the emergency services."

"True. But you are a survivor, Motts." Osian continued to hold the card out to her. "Bit old-fashioned to have these. Just easier when someone doesn't want to give you their phone number. Take it. Paper doesn't bite."

"Surviving serves solitary…."

"Sabbaticals?" Osian suggested.

"Surviving serves solitary sabbaticals." Motts took the card from him. She ran her finger along the letters. It was nice and simple with the basic information for the group. "Still not a firefighter or a paramedic or a police officer."

"You're an amateur detective." Osian smiled when she glanced up from the card. "I meant what I said. You'd be more than welcome. So when do you head back to Cornwall?"

"After Boxing Day, maybe. Before the New Year. I haven't decided quite yet. Mum hopes never." Motts shuddered at the idea of being stuck in her childhood home again. Constantly feeling like a failure. Being trapped. "Definitely sooner rather than later."

"How about after Christmas? You come up to visit again? We'd love to have you on the podcast. Talk about your experiences in Cornwall. Maybe sneak in a visit with the therapy group?" Osian tapped his finger against the card in her hand. "Think about it and let me know? Dannel never likes to do things last minute, so if you want more time, I'm sure this isn't the only chance we'll have."

"Thank you."

"From one amateur detective to another, from one survivor to another, you'll be all right." Osian offered her a gentle smile. "You've got good friends around you. Dempsey's not a bad bloke. Less perpetually annoyed than our resident detective inspector."

"Perpetual. Good word." Motts repeated it a few times under her breath. "We should go inside before Cactus worries about me."

"We wouldn't want that." Osian didn't sound like he was teasing her, but Motts narrowed her eyes at him just the same. "I never underestimate a naked cat in a cardigan."

CHAPTER ELEVEN

December twenty-third.

Motts had woken up with Cactus poking her in the cheek. Repeatedly. "Yes, yes, I am fully aware that we're going to be late for breakfast. You won't seem so eager when Mum is telling me about how I should change your diet."

Meow.

Cactus was, as always, unbothered by anything aside from his snacks, his cuddles, and his morning walk.

"We're going back to Mum and Dad's today." Motts forced herself out of bed and into a change of clothes. *Meow.* "I'm not exactly thrilled by this turn of events either."

Standing by the window, Motts stared out onto

the street below. She spotted the unmarked police vehicle parked down the road. *We should bring them tea or coffee. Definitely coffee. How long have they sat outside in the cold?*

"How's the head, Mottsy?" Vina greeted her when she finally made it downstairs with Cactus trailing after her. "We've got toast, lemon curd, tea and coffee, plus Osian mentioned you might want a few paracetamol this morning if you're still achy from your fall."

"My head remains attached to my body." Motts brought her hand up to gingerly touch the small lump left behind from hitting the stairs. "Think my mum will notice?"

"Yes, about that." River tried to hide behind Nish, who laughed at him.

"What've you done?" Motts gratefully accepted the chai latte Vina handed to her. They'd obviously brought tea from home with them. "River."

"I couldn't lie when Dad asked me what happened to you. It's possible he then told your dad," River admitted. "Sorry."

"Brilliant." Motts slumped into one of the kitchen chairs with a groan. "Going to need more than paracetamol. Mum's going to be insufferable."

"Back in a mo, need to check on my mum." River

dashed out of the room. Her cousin was way too much of a morning person at times, especially when on holiday.

Her mum had a history of overreacting to the slightest injury. She treated Motts like a child even after she'd grown up. Moving to Polperro hadn't helped like everyone claimed it would. If anything, she'd gotten even more dramatic.

"If you eat your toast any slower, you might actually work off every single calorie from it before you finish the meal," Vina teased. "How have you managed half a piece in ten minutes?"

"Prolonging the inevitable." Nish refilled Motts's latte for her. "Chin up. We'll swing by to visit. Your dad's already invited all of us over for Christmas Eve and the day itself."

Motts wanted to stay with her friends. Spend the rest of the week with them instead of returning to the misery of overwhelming expectations and disappointments. "Can you wrap up a few of those pastries for me? Make another mug of coffee? I want to take breakfast out to the poor person who had to watch the house all night."

"Did you hear?" River came bounding back into the room from seeing his parents. He set a plate of baos in front of them. "Mum made breakfast sausage buns."

Motts immediately grabbed one for herself. Auntie Lily made the best breakfast bao—a fusion of their British and Chinese heritages. She stood up when Nish returned with the coffee and a plate for the police officer outside. "I'll be back in a minute."

Making sure Cactus stayed inside was tricky with her hands full, but Motts managed it. She walked across the street toward the parked vehicle; the man inside lowered the window when she approached.

"Hello." Motts held out the mug and plate. "Not sure if it's allowed, but we wanted to bring you breakfast. I'm Motts."

"Detective Inspector Milo Dorsey. Ta for this." He took the mug and plate. "Everything all right inside?"

"Normal levels of chaos." Motts shoved her hands into the pockets of her cardigan. "Were you here all night? Sounds very boring."

"Detective inspector work isn't all dead bodies and excitement." He took a bite of one of the baos. "This is delicious. Cheers for the breakfast."

"Aren't you part of DCI Byrne's cold case unit? Isn't that *all* dead bodies?"

"You make an excellent point." He saluted her with a mug of coffee.

"I'm going back to my parents' house. Are you following?" Motts had no idea if there was some sort of protocol when dealing with an unofficial official police detail. "Should I give you the address?"

"DCI Byrne's planning to swing by soon. I imagine he'll go with you, then decide what happens next." Dorsey finished up the baos and offered Motts the empty plate. He sipped the coffee. "I can bring this back when I'm done."

"Have you learnt anything new about…."

Dorsey held a hand up, causing her to trail off midsentence. "I don't have any updates. You'll have to wait for DCI Byrne."

It had been worth a try. Motts was dying to know if they'd discovered anything from Hugo or Jonty. *Not dying. Definitely not dying. I'm living to know.*

Living doesn't sound right.

"Are you okay?" Dorsey drew Motts out of her thoughts.

"Yes, sorry. We'll probably leave in an hour or so." Motts decided she'd had enough conversation with a stranger and spun around to head into the house.

I should've said bye.

It wound up being closer to two hours before

Motts finally climbed into Vina's car. Detective Inspector Dorsey waved when they drove past him. He quickly followed.

A text message had also arrived from Dempsey, which explained he would come by her parents' house to talk over what they'd discovered. Something for her to look forward to. She wasn't holding out hope for anything else pleasant to happen.

Vina found a space to park down the road from her parents'. She grabbed Motts's hand. "Mottsy? Why don't we get all your things and go back to Cornwall? The village is lovely at Christmas. Marnie makes the best gingerbread biscuits. Doc always delivers shortbread with the post."

"I can't."

"You could." Vina wiggled her eyebrows. "They can't actually stop us from leaving."

"It's Christmas. You're supposed to spend it with family." Motts did find the idea of hiding away from everyone appealing. She could always count on Vina to encourage her to take care of herself before anything else. "Sometimes, you have to endure frustration because it's the right thing to do."

"Fine. But just say the word, and it's jailbreak time."

"We're not in prison. And you have to stop

watching all those shows on Netflix." Motts was incredibly grateful for her friends. They went above and beyond what most people would do. "I'm really glad you're in my life."

"Stop. Don't make me weepy. I've a date later." Vina swiped at a non-existent tear. "All right, I suppose I should drop you off."

Easing back onto the road, Vina continued on until they arrived. Motts broke into a smile when she spotted her grandparents' vehicle parked out front. She hadn't known if they'd be coming for certain; her gran didn't always do so well trapped in a car for hours at a time.

"Hello, poppet." Her granddad greeted her when she got out of the vehicle. Cactus immediately went up to him. "And hello to you too, young man. Have you been taking care of our Pineapple?"

"How was the drive?" Motts rushed over to give him a hug. "How's Gran?"

"Your gran is inside taking over the holiday preparations, so your mum will likely be in quite the mood." Her granddad chuckled. He shifted his hold on Cactus. "Now, what's this I hear about you taking a tumble down the stairs?"

"I was shoved." Motts glanced over her shoulder

to where Vina was carrying over her bag. "Run while you still can. Mum's in a mood."

"Right." Vina handed the bag to Motts, gave both her and her granddad a quick hug, and kissed Cactus on the head. "Must run. Don't want to be late for my date."

"It's not even eleven in the morning. Your date is this evening." Motts laughed when Vina practically ran back to her car and took off. "She's so brave."

"Not sure we can judge, since we're hiding outside in the cold." Her granddad gave her another squeeze. "Why don't we sneak around to the garden? I left the gate open."

"What about Gran? I have to say hello." Motts found herself being guided toward the garden gate despite her protests. Cactus was busy cuddling with her granddad. "I'd say he's missed you."

"He's a good young man, yes he is. How about you, poppet? How are you doing?"

Motts shrugged. "Been worse."

"We'll get some of your gran's scones in you. And a fresh pot of tea. It'll cure what ails you." He smiled down at Cactus. "Your dad's got his firepit going. It's lovely and warm."

"Brilliant." Motts knew her mum would likely stay inside the house. She hadn't approved of the firepit that her dad had added to the garden a few years ago. "Certainly chilly enough for a December morning."

"Happy almost Christmas, poppet."

It occurred to Motts while sitting by the fire in the garden that most people would be home on December twenty-third. Aside from the last-minute shoppers. She thought it might be the perfect time to chat with Mrs Ceresto's neighbours.

Someone had surely seen something. The pale blue car, maybe. The absurdly tall Barbrow brothers. One or both. Motts didn't know if both or just one were involved in the murders.

She'd assumed Hugo, the elder, was responsible. Jonty had been too young when Jenny died. Hadn't he?

It made her wonder how young did a serial killer start their murderous journey. Motts vaguely recalled hearing about one who'd begun around the age of twelve. Someone had mentioned it on a podcast.

Jonty hadn't been that much younger. Had he been the killer? Or Hugo? Were they both involved? Had siblings ever been serial killers together?

Could murder run in families?

I need to see Mrs Ceresto's house. Speak with her neighbours. Her death has to be linked to everything else.

What else could it be?

I'm going to need a ride.

And an accomplice.

"Granddad." Motts caught his attention where he'd been dozing by the fire with Cactus on his chest. "Want to go for a drive with me?"

"A drive?" he asked without opening his eyes. "Perhaps to pay our respects to your former teacher? They're having a service for her today, according to your mother."

"Are they?" Motts hadn't heard. Funerals did tend to bring out loads of people. "I'd planned to go by her house, but… is it rude to crash a funeral?"

"You're simply a former student who wants to pay her respects." He sat up slowly and smiled at her. A grumbly Cactus was dislodged from his sleeping spot. "Shall we poke our noses into the investigation?"

Somehow, they managed to sneak away from the house without Motts having been confronted by her mum. She knew it was only delaying the inevitable. They were bound to have words at some point.

Lots of unpleasant words.

While her granddad drove, Motts used her phone

to search for information about her teacher. Instead, she found an online memorial started by another student. Someone from her last class before Mrs Ceresto had retired from the school.

Mrs Ceresto had been a widow. No children; at least, none were mentioned in the memorial. She'd had a caretaker who lived with her.

Interesting.

Where had her caretaker been when she'd been drowned in the bath?

Caretaker callously circumvents—

What's a good C-word?

CHAPTER TWELVE

THE FUNERAL SERVICE MADE MOTTS SAD. ONLY A handful of people showed up at the church. Probably a good thing, given the size of the place.

Tiny churches lent themselves well to small services.

"Not much of a turnout." Her granddad sat with her in the back of the little chapel. "Us. The reverend. Plus four others."

The service had just finished. Motts had decided to wait to see if anyone stayed behind for a few minutes. She wished Vina had come with her, since she tended to do so well getting information from people.

"Sad. I wonder if she had any family." Motts

recognised one of the people sitting in front of them. "I think he used to be our physical education teacher."

"Why don't you say hello?" Her granddad nudged her when the man walked past them toward the exit. "I'll chat with the reverend. See what I can find out."

Gathering up her courage and rehearsing a casual hello in her head, Motts squeezed by her granddad and followed the man outside. She couldn't for the life of her remember his name. *Mr Edwards? Ellis? Elliot?* It had started with an E.

"Hello," Motts called out to him when she finally stepped out into the fresh air. "You taught at my school."

Oh yes, casual greeting. Well done.

He frowned at her while attempting to tug on a pair of gloves. "Did I? Surprised to see a former student here. Not many kept in touch with the old bat."

Motts blinked at him in surprise. *Rude. Ruddy rudeness runs rampant.* "Mr…."

"Mr Tellier."

So, not E.

"I'm—"

"The fruit girl. I remember you. Apricot?"

"Pineapple." Motts tried not to glower at him.

Apricot? Who calls their daughter apricot? Okay. In fair-ness, who calls their daughter Pineapple? My mum. "Pineapple Mottley. Were you close with Mrs Ceresto?"

"A little. I live in the house adjacent to hers." He finally got his second glove on his hand. "How did you hear about her death?"

"I was paying her a visit the morning of the fire. So I called the police." Motts shoved her hands into her pockets. The weather had turned even colder than when she'd woken up. "Did you see anything?"

"I wasn't home."

"Did you happen to see a pale blue car in the days leading up to the fire?" Motts tried for casual, but she sounded stilted even to her ears.

"Maybe a week prior? Why?"

"Just curious." Motts shrugged awkwardly.

"Right." He started to walk away.

"Did you know Hugo Barbrow?" Motts's question stopped him in his tracks.

"Barbrow? Jonathan was in my class. I remember him quite vividly." Her former teacher seemed uneasy all of a sudden. "Was Hugo his brother? I never knew his name. I had no end of trouble with both of them, though. I reprimanded Jonathan once."

"You remember it even now?" Motts figured over

the years, as a teacher, he must've told off hundreds of students.

"I'll never forget the Barbrows. I found the entrails of some animal spread over my car the following morning. The authorities never found out who." Mr Tellier shivered violently. "My neighbour had a pet go missing the day before. The police let the matter rest. I knew it was them."

"How?" Motts held her breath for the answer.

"They told me. Or, Jonathan, the younger brother, asked me during class if I enjoyed raw meat." Mr Tellier peered over her shoulder toward the church. "Come to think of it, he had problems with Mrs Ceresto as well."

"Oh?"

"She used to tell him off constantly for trying to get into the girls' classes." He went down a couple of the steps in front of the church. "Must be off. Pineapple?"

"Yes?" Motts decided not to correct him on her preferred name. Why bother?

"I'd leave the Barbrows alone. I can't imagine they're any less dangerous now than they were as young lads." Mr Tellier walked away from her, tugging his coat tighter around his frame.

They're certainly more dangerous now.

Or equally dangerous.

"Everything all right, poppet?" Her granddad found her standing outside, shivering in the cold and staring down the road where Mr Tellier had gone. "Did something happen?"

"Mr Tellier, my old physical education teacher." Motts followed her granddad down the steps toward his car. "He had a run-in with the Barbrows back when I was a student. Did you discover anything interesting?"

"The brunette in the church happened to be Mrs Ceresto's live-in caretaker. We're having tea with her in an hour." Her granddad grinned at her when her eyes widened in surprise. "I can be rather charming."

"Rather charming? Gran would say you're a cheeky sod." Motts slipped into the passenger's seat, grateful to be out of the cold breeze. She reached into her pocket for her phone and paused when she spotted the pale blue Nissan directly across the road. "Bugger."

"Where on earth did you learn that sort of language?"

"You?" Motts scrambled to get her phone into recording mode. She managed to get a quick video before the Nissan took off. "Berk."

"Friend of yours?"

"Not exactly. Why don't we poke around Mrs Ceresto's lane while we wait for tea?" Motts attached the video she'd filmed to a text to Dempsey. She included a summary of what Mr Tellier had told her. "Gran's going to think we abandoned her."

"She'll be just fine."

While her granddad drove, Motts sent a second message to her group chat with the video and conversation. She figured they'd all want to know. It took her a moment to realise someone had added Osian and Dannel to the chat.

The group chat debated what questions Motts should ask the caretaker. Dempsey asked her to be careful and stick with her granddad. He planned to put the protective detail back on her; they'd be waiting at her parents' house.

He doesn't need to know we're not heading straight there.

Her granddad found a parking space on the street across from Mrs Ceresto's home. Motts didn't want to get out into the cold. She frowned at a scruffy young man in the front garden of the house next to her teacher's.

"Problem, poppet?"

"We saw him the day of the fire. He barged by

Vina and me." Motts climbed out of the car and shoved her hands immediately into her pockets to keep them warm. "Ready to be charming?"

"Always." He followed her across the street.

The caution tape had been removed already from Mrs Ceresto's house. Motts noticed the neighbour watching them, so she decided not to play coy. They walked right up to his front gate.

"Morning." Her granddad waved cheerfully at him. "Bit of a miserable day for it, isn't it?"

Day for what? Why do people say that? What's the "it"? They never give one.

A nice day for skipping? Hiking? Doing absolutely sod all?

While Motts debated internally, her granddad introduced the both of them. She tuned back into the conversation in time to catch his name. *Geoff Dixon.* Up close to the man, she realised he was much younger than she'd thought, probably in his early twenties.

"I saw you." He came up to lean against his gate. "When her house went up, bumped into you and your friend. Sorry about that. I was rushing back to the hospital. My nan's there. I've been taking care of her house while she's there."

"Sorry to hear about your nan. Is she all right?" Her granddad always handled conversations far more naturally than Motts.

"Not sure. The doctor's still trying to sort out what's wrong with her. I spend most of my nights with her, then take a break while my mum's there during the day." Geoff sighed. "Did you know Mrs Ceresto?"

"She was my teacher in primary school." Motts looped her arm around her granddad's. "I'd planned to visit with her the day of the fire."

"Terrible thing." He shook his head. "I heard police say she died in the middle of the night. Wish I'd been home to help her."

"Did you see anything odd in the last week or so? A blue Nissan? Or any strangers in the area?" Motts asked. *Subtle. Real. Subtle.*

"I did see a tall bloke down the street a few times. I even caught him on camera trying to get into her back garden a few days before the fire. Of course, I showed the police." Geoff gripped his gate, frowning at her. "What's your interest?"

"Just… curious," Motts said unconvincingly. "I suppose I feel connected with my teacher. I'd come to see her, after all."

Geoff was silent while Motts fidgeted in front of

him. Her granddad began to speak but was interrupted. "Want to see the video? Police didn't recognise him, but you might."

The video didn't have the best quality. Motts clearly spotted the grainy figure trying to climb the garden fence. A light popped on, and the man scurried out of view, likely spooked by Geoff coming outside.

No view of the intruder's face. The only thing Motts noticed was his height. Tall. Very tall, by the ease with which he'd climbed into Geoff's garden and had been about to go into Mrs Ceresto's. He had to be one of the Barbrows.

How many incredibly tall murderous types strolled around Dulwich?

"Did you recognise him?" Geoff asked after turning off the tablet where he'd shown them the video.

"I don't know." Motts didn't want to give him any details. Dempsey wouldn't appreciate her sharing anything about the case with a random stranger. "You showed the detectives?"

"I showed the first copper who knocked on my door. He wasn't interested." Geoff shrugged.

Motts dug out a notepad from her backpack. She scribbled down Dempsey's email address and ripped the paper to hand to Geoff. "Send it here. He's the DCI in charge of the case. He'll be interested. I promise."

"Cheers." Geoff grabbed the paper.

"Hope your nan improves soon." Motts waved goodbye, then walked away with her granddad.

"What do you think, poppet?"

"I don't know." Motts thought the figure on the video was one of the brothers. But which one? "I just don't know."

"Shall we see if we're too early for tea?"

"It's never too early for tea." Motts wanted to see if the caretaker, Janice Sallow, had any details to add about the day of the fire. "The firefighters must've managed to clean up the place if she's still living there."

"She claimed to live in a small flat in the back of the garden. One of those wee houses, I think," her granddad explained. "Allowed her some privacy while being close enough to care for her client, I suppose."

"Interesting." Motts hadn't noticed a tiny house in the garden. She'd been too focused on the shadowy figure in the video. "I wonder if Mrs Ceresto was her only client."

"I don't think so. She mentioned being out the

day of the fire because she'd gone to see another elderly client a few streets over." Her granddad had definitely charmed answers out of Janice Sallow.

"The police should take you on all of their interrogations."

"Call me PC Mottley." Her granddad chuckled. "Are you ready, poppet?"

"Not really." Motts had come to a stop on the pavement. The smell of damp smoke still lingered in the air. She closed her eyes and breathed in deeply. It didn't help. If anything, the icy fear inside her grew. "I can't. Can't. Granddad."

"All right, poppet. I'm walking you back to the car. You'll sit in warmth. Get your headphones out. I'll get the radio going to some of the dreadful holiday music. You rest. I'll pop in to speak with the caretaker." Her granddad guided her back to his vehicle and forced her into the passenger's seat. "You lock the doors. Okay?"

Motts managed to nod. Her brain had momentarily shut down, and words were next to impossible. She hated the feeling of not being able to put a sentence together.

"Right." Her granddad grabbed her backpack. "Forgive the intrusion, poppet."

He fished around for her headphones and gently

eased them onto her head. Motts reached up to turn them on to the highest level of noise cancellation. It offered at least a partial relief.

I want to go home to Cornwall.

Sod Christmas in Dulwich and serial killing berks.

CHAPTER THIRTEEN

"Why don't you stay out here for a while? I'll keep everyone distracted while you enjoy the peace and quiet." Her granddad patted her hand gently and headed into the house.

Slumping further into the seat, Motts peered out the window at her parents' front garden. Immaculate, as always. Her mum had exacting standards when it came to the outward appearance of their home.

The drive across Dulwich had been a silent one. Her granddad, bless him, was content to let her simply be. She'd slowly started to feel better.

A tap on the car window scared her half to death. Motts placed a hand over her heart while reaching down to lower the window. She glared at Dempsey, who stood smiling at her.

Note to self: stop panicking over every random, unexpected sound.

"Dorsey mentioned you'd sat out here for ten minutes." Dempsey stepped back to let her get out of the car. "He worried. I worried, and here I am."

"You worried because I sat in my car?" Motts knew it was odd but not strange enough to be concerning. She never quite knew how non-autistics viewed things. "Or have I missed something in the translation?"

"I worried because you went to your teacher's funeral, which had to be difficult to process emotionally." Dempsey continued when she shifted uncomfortably but didn't respond. "You've had a narrow miss with a killer. Several narrow misses. You had to deal with people. And you're about to be stuck in a house with family, including your mum, who tends to cause you immense levels of stress. So I can't *imagine* why you'd want to lock yourself away in a car."

"Sarcasm?"

"Only the last bit," Dempsey clarified with a gentle smile. "Not sure I can resolve any of those problems for you. I could arrest your mum."

"She'd attack you with her duster." Motts couldn't help bursting out laughing at the visual in her mind. "Is there a specific subset of the law dealing with crimes of the goose feather variety?"

"I shall endeavour to create one if there isn't, if only to write a report with the words 'goose feather crimes' on it," Dempsey promised with a grin.

"Some days, I wonder if you're overly loquacious just for the fun of it." Motts slipped her hands into her pockets. The temperature had continued to drop. "Did you speak with Geoff Dixon? He showed me the video."

"I've seen it." Dempsey nodded.

"Tall bloke." Motts wondered if they'd determined the exact height of the figure on the video. She'd heard of that being done before.

"Very. We couldn't determine the exact height, but either of the brothers would fit." He answered the question she hadn't even asked yet. "Have any plans for Christmas Eve?"

"Not dying?" Motts's laugh felt hollow to her own ears. "Try not to run afoul of my mum."

"Watch the goose feathers."

She decided not to dignify his bad joke with anything more than rolling her eyes. "How about you?"

"Sadly, working. Cases won't solve themselves, and I haven't a family to spend the day with." He shrugged indifferently.

"We have lunch at one on Christmas Eve, then Mum insists on watching the same films. I usually disappear into the garden with spiked hot chocolate." Motts peered up at him. "Be here at noon. You can walk with my granddad and me. It's our tradition."

"Motts."

"Don't bring food. Mum gets annoyed when people do." Motts waved, then jogged up the path to the house. "Cactus will miss you if you don't show up."

Shutting the door behind her, Motts hoped he would come. If nothing else, it provided a distraction for her mum. Anything to help her get through the madness of the holidays with her family.

"Hello, poppet." Her dad stepped out of his study down the hall. He watched her remove her coat and bend down to pick up Cactus, who'd come rushing up. "You'll be pleased to know your granddad has your mum searching the attic."

"Why?"

"Claims she's lost a family heirloom." Her dad seemed greatly amused.

"We don't have family heirlooms," Motts pointed out.

"Hence why I'm hiding in my study. Want to join me?"

"Are all families this strange?" Motts followed him down the hall into his study with Cactus perched on her shoulder. "Or just ours?"

"I shall assume your question is rhetorical and answer anyway. Not just ours. Every family has its own brand of bizarre." Her dad returned to the ridiculously comfortable chair that sat by the fire in his study. Motts had considered stealing it on several occasions. "Your mum wants you to sell the cottage."

"Dad."

"Forewarned is forearmed." He offered a smile, then picked up his book and returned to reading.

With a sigh, Motts decided to leave him to it. Her father was lovely but ineffectual when the situation involved dealing with her mum. At least she'd have backup in the form of her grandparents.

"In from the cold, are you, sweetheart?" Her gran poked her head out of the kitchen. "Fancy a mince pie? I've a fresh batch out of the oven."

A mince pie turned into a stack of them along with a pot of tea. Motts disappeared into her bedroom with her bounty. Cactus immediately leapt off her shoulder to burrow on her pillow.

"Have you missed me?" Motts set her bounty on her nightstand and grabbed her phone from her backpack. She sent a quick update to their group chat. "Mum's going to be on the rampage later, Cactus. I'd wager she'll figure out there was no heirloom in the attic soon enough."

Meow.

"Yes, Granddad is the absolute best." Motts moved the plate of mince pies out of Cactus's reach when he decided to inspect them. "Not an approved snack."

Sitting on the beanbag in the corner of her room, Motts sipped tea and went over her day in her mind. The more she considered the video footage Geoff Dixon had shown her, the more she was convinced the figure had been Jonty. And not Hugo. She had no proof at all.

It was simply a feeling.

Dempsey couldn't arrest either Hugo or Jonty based on her feeling. Pity. She wished the CCTV footage had been clearer.

Feelings frequently fluctuate floundering facts.

"There you are, darling." Her mother came into her room without even knocking on the door. She paused to offer a disapproving glance at the plate on the nightstand. "Your auntie and uncle should be here within the hour. Why aren't you ready?"

"Ready for what? I had no idea we had people coming over. I'm not a clairvoyant." Motts hadn't heard anything from her cousin about them coming by to eat. They usually waited until Christmas Eve to get together. "Hasn't Gran taken up residence in the kitchen?"

"Why are you snacking? Did your father sneak those to you?" Her mum went over to grab the plate, but Motts got there first.

She snagged one of the pies and shoved it into her mouth, needing the fortification. "I've invited DCI Byrne to lunch tomorrow."

"Pineapple."

"Mother." Motts had no intentions of backing down now. She'd already made the invitation. "It would be rude to cancel. He's excited."

Doubtful.

Lying liar lists lies.

"Ah, poppet. Your gran needs you in the kitchen." Her granddad waved from the doorway, gesturing for her to follow. He winked when she went by him with Cactus on her heels. "Ah, hello dear, did you find the missing platter?"

Coughing quickly to cover her laugh, Motts went to find her gran in the kitchen. Flour was everywhere, with trays of treats in various processes of completion. She immediately washed her hands and went to work decorating some of the biscuits.

"Poppet? Your young man is here." Her granddad joined them in the kitchen halfway through her second batch of cookies. He snatched one off a plate, narrowly avoiding a playful swat from her gran. "He's waiting outside. Off you go."

My young man?

"You are not young." Motts blurted the words when she found Dempsey waiting by her front door. She covered her face to hide a blush and groaned. "Sorry."

"Did your granddad tell you a young man was waiting for you?" Dempsey hazarded a guess.

Motts thought his smile seemed forced. He was on edge. Stressed. More than he'd been when he'd popped by earlier. "What's happened? Did you find the Barbrows?"

"No." Dempsey took a step closer to her. "You spoke with one of your teachers at the funeral? Nathan Tellier?"

"Yes?" Motts had a terrible feeling in her stomach. "I mean, yes. I did. I told you. Texted you all the details. He had a run-in with Hugo and Jonty."

"He's had two now."

"Oh no. Is he—" Motts couldn't bring herself to say the words.

"Not dead. Badly injured in the hospital. I can't give you all the details." Dempsey held up a hand to stop her from speaking. "Not because I won't, but I don't have them."

"Did he see who did it?" Motts asked.

"He's not in a position to tell us much of anything. However, a neighbour spotted him unconscious in his garden." Dempsey glanced over to the right at the window where her mother could be seen observing them surreptitiously while dusting the ornaments. He waved at her, making Motts laugh. "The neighbour happens to be a security specialist. They have cameras on every corner of their house. I've got two detectives going through the footage now."

"No witnesses?"

Dempsey narrowed his eyes on her, then finally nodded. "One. Not to the attack itself, but I can't share details. We did receive a general description fitting Jonathan Barbrow."

"Jonty?" Motts had thought the older brother

more likely the killer given his age at the time of the first murder. "Jonty. Not Hugo."

"In this instance, at least. It doesn't rule out Hugo in all of the killings," Dempsey cautioned. "We're keeping the constable stationed outside of the house. Just being overly cautious. Let them know if you're going out. Please be careful."

"I always try to be careful. Things often go awry without my doing anything at all." Motts hazarded a look at the window to find her mother still pretending to rearrange the various decorations. "She's being decidedly odd. More than usual."

"Maybe she wants a better look at your young man?" Dempsey chuckled. His smile faded when a horn honked behind them. He turned and waved at DI Dorsey, who'd parked behind her granddad's car. "I'd never attempt to dissuade you from using your investigative abilities. You've a cleverer mind than you give yourself credit for."

"Thank you?"

"Try not to go alone. Give my poor constable the location you plan to be. And keep your phone on you. At all times." Dempsey dug into his pocket and pulled out a bracelet with a square charm. "This is a panic button. It connects to an app we'll put on your phone. The second you press it, I will get a text along with four other people you select. It'll give us GPS coordinates of where you are."

Motts didn't know how to react to the bracelet. She held her hand out for it. "You think this is necessary?"

"Think? I'm aware of the numerous times you've been perilously close to being seriously injured by cold-blooded killers."

"Technically, aren't all killers warm-blooded? Is it even possible for a human to have cold blood? If you put yourself in a freezer, will your blood be cold?" Motts wondered absently. "Right. Sorry. Not what you meant. Oh, wait, I have a present for you in case you don't come by tomorrow."

Without giving him a chance to respond, Motts darted back into the house. She ignored her mum and searched through the presents under the tree to find the right one. A bemused Dempsey stood waiting for her return.

"Roget's Thesaurus?"

"First edition. Granddad found it for me. Words. All the words. Fancy ones as well." Motts hoped her gift hadn't upset him. "Happy Christmas?"

"Thank you." His smile seemed genuine enough, and Motts relaxed. He hadn't been insulted by her gift. "It's brilliant. Unexpected but brilliant—much like you are."

"Brilliant but unexpected." Motts carefully put the bracelet on her wrist. She gingerly touched the panic button, careful not to accidentally set the thing off. "I've had worse assessments."

CHAPTER FOURTEEN

"Motts. Wake up."

"You are not five years old anymore." Motts peered at the clock on her nightstand before glaring at her cousin, who had crept into her bedroom. "Why are you waking up at six in the morning?

"Plans, Motts. Plans." River set a mug on the nightstand. He flicked on the lamp. "Fancy an adventure?"

"At six in the morning?" Motts sat up slowly, dislodging Cactus, who grumbled at both of them, then vanished underneath the blankets. "What sort of adventure?"

"You missed this last night when you and Vina snuck upstairs to gossip." River sat on the edge of her bed.

"Missed what?" Motts sipped her coffee in the hopes of finding the patience to deal with the early morning and her cousin's antics.

"Your dad remembered Hugo and Jonty's parents. Remembered they originally lived a few streets over, not far from one of the entrances to the woods." River nudged her leg. "Nish had the idea—"

"Nish?" Motts interrupted. "Nish had an idea? Not you or Vina?"

"Okay, fine, I had the idea." River bumped her leg for a second time. "Drink up. We want to sneak out before your parents are awake."

"So not five, but teenagers once again?" Motts continued drinking her coffee and listened to their half-baked plan to take an early morning stroll around the Barbrows' old neighbourhood and venture into the woods. "Why is this an amazing idea? Fairly confident our detective inspector friends would say it was the absolute worst."

"You have a panic button." He grabbed the bracelet from her nightstand, where it rested next to her phone. "See? We can even call for help. Aren't you the least bit curious about where they lived?"

"They don't live there now." Motts didn't think they'd learn anything when the Barbrows had moved ages ago. "Is there breakfast?"

"Curry English Breakfast Baos. Mum made them last night. We can sneak a bunch of them." River dragged her blanket off her and dodged Cactus, who swiped at him. "Oi. Be nice. I bought you presents."

"How'd you get into the house without waking everyone?" Motts assumed they'd all headed back to their Airbnb for the night.

"Granddad. He was up when we got here. Wants to come with since it's an easy walk from here." River snickered when she groaned. "Hurry up. We're waiting downstairs."

"What exactly are you expecting us to find?" Motts slowly climbed out of bed. She helped Cactus get resituated in the blankets.

"No idea." River slipped out of her room and quietly closed her door.

No idea.

No idea.

Of course they have no idea.

What exactly are we going to see at six in the morning when it's dark outside?

Nothing.

Despite her thoughts, Motts found herself getting dressed for the earliest walk she'd ever had on Christmas Eve. Her granddad greeted her with a cheery hug. He held his arm out for her to take;

despite her sigh of reluctance, she couldn't help returning his grin when he handed her a torch.

"I sincerely hope this isn't a new holiday tradition." Nish seemed as unenthused as Motts at being dragged out of the cosy warmth of bed. "Why couldn't we take this walk later? In the daylight?"

"It's already twilight. We've got a hint of light," her granddad pointed out while they continued down the street. "Here we come a-wassailing…."

With a sigh of resignation, Motts joined in with her granddad and cousin. They sang their way along the path leading into the next street that connected to Dulwich Woods. She hoped they didn't annoy anyone with their singing.

Anyone aside from herself.

"Your mum did want you to go carolling," Vina teased when they finally stopped singing.

"I have carolled against my will." Motts stowed the torch in her coat pocket. She wondered if they should've given the constable a heads-up about their morning adventure. "Carolling conventions conveniently crushes."

"Seven out of ten." Vina checked her phone when it gave a jaunty tune. "Taara wishes us good luck. She's stuck at Heathrow waiting for her parents to arrive."

The first issue they found was none of them knew which specific house had been the Barbrows'. The second came from what Motts had already questioned. So what did they gain from staring at a former residence?

Nothing.

Frozen fingers and toes. And probably a cold. Motts ventured toward the end of the lane and the little path leading into the woods. She didn't know what she was searching for, but something drew her closer.

Moving off the well-defined path, Motts found a slender trail. Not well walked. She had expected the others to follow her.

Assumed.

Assumptions could often be so hazardous. Motts had delved deeper into the woods before realizing they hadn't. *I do not enjoy being lost in the woods this early in the morning. At all.*

It was only Dulwich. She'd spent a fair amount of time in the ancient forest growing up. So how had she gotten disoriented so quickly?

Panicking. That was how she'd gotten disoriented. Motts leaned against the nearest tree trunk and forced herself to calm down. She tried her phone, but service had always been spotty in the woods.

Right.

I'm in the woods, might as well keep going.

The trail led into one of the denser parts of the woods. Motts stepped through a small cluster of trees to find a clearing. She shone the torch around; it was definitely man-made.

Someone had gone out of their way to create a hidden clearing in the middle of the woods. Motts noticed a hollow in the large tree in the centre of the area. She crouched down to get a better look and couldn't believe her eyes.

Holy mother of mittens.

I hope my panic button works even without decent service on my mobile.

Jamming the button on her bracelet, Motts continued to inspect what she'd found. She tried to avoid touching anything. Dempsey wouldn't appreciate her fingerprints being all over his evidence.

After propping her torch to provide better lighting, Motts grabbed her phone. She wanted a video of everything before the police arrived. Of the melted candles. The laminated photos. Newspaper articles. There were random pieces of jewellery hung from hooks dug into the inside of the trunk.

On closer inspection, Motts noticed tool marks along the wood. Whoever had created this shrine had expanded on a naturally occurring hollow. They'd made this space for themselves.

All of the panic that had bled away came rushing back like a tidal wave. Motts grabbed her phone and tried to place a call. None of her attempts connected, no matter who she tried.

If my phone isn't working, will the panic button?

Note to self: Ask essential questions before potentially dangerous situations—not after you're in the middle of one.

Grabbing the torch, Motts tried to get a closer view of some of the photos. Her heart stopped when she spotted Jenny's as the highest one. All the others were spread out underneath.

Rows of photos of her classmates.

A shiver went up her spine that had nothing to do with the crisp December weather. Motts stumbled away from the tree. She didn't want to stare into the faces of her former classmates—most of whom had been murdered.

"Motts."

Her cousin's shout drew her attention. Motts grabbed her torch and began flashing it in intervals into the woods. She waved it back and forth, hoping it would draw their attention better than calling out to them.

She tried. Her voice didn't want to work. River's name came out as more of a whisper, which wasn't helpful to any of them.

"Motts? Keep shining your light. I've got the police with me." River's voice came closer. He eventually popped into the little clearing and rushed over to her. "Hug?"

"Not at the moment. Sorry." Motts didn't think she could take being grabbed by anyone. Not with how shaken she was by her discovery. "I found… something?"

"There you are." Dempsey pushed through the bushes to join them, followed by Nish and DI Dorsey. "Are you okay?"

"I—" Motts didn't know how to explain. She gestured with the torch toward the hollowed-out tree. "I got a little disoriented, and then I stumbled upon this shrine. I tried texting, but it didn't work, so the panic button seemed the next option."

Heading over to the tree, Dempsey bent down as she had. He shone his own torch around, taking in the photos, articles, and trophies from the victims. Motts stepped further to the side when he called out to Dorsey to join him.

The detectives had a hushed conversation by the tree. Dempsey finally stood back up. He came over to her while Dorsey began talking into his radio, requesting a forensics team and several other members of the cold case unit.

"How'd you even find this? And did you touch anything in the tree?" Dempsey asked. He clicked off the torch, since sunlight had finally begun to pierce the forest.

"I tried not to touch anything." Motts had gone out of her way to make sure her fingerprints wouldn't mess up the investigation. "I found a little trail leading away from one of the main paths. It's how I got lost in the first place. I've never been this way in the woods, despite having walked here a fair amount."

"We're going to lead you out of the woods and make sure you get home safely. DI Dorsey will wait here to ensure no one messes with the shrine." Dempsey stepped away to speak with his detective once again. "It's going to be all right. Let's get you somewhere warm."

Motts shivered when the wind cut through the trees. "Is it too soon to say I told you this would be a disaster?"

"In fairness, I had no way of predicting you'd find

a creepy serial killer treehouse in the middle of Dulwich Wood." River grabbed his gloves out of his pocket to offer her. "Want to warm your hands up?"

Motts touched a hand to his gloves to make sure the fabric didn't bother her skin. It didn't, so she took them from him gratefully. She'd started to lose feeling in the tips of her fingers. "You haven't told Mum, have you?"

"We hadn't gotten the chance to tell anyone else when the police came up the lane in full force. It was impressive. Granddad and Nish have gone back to your parents' house to delay and distract in the hopes you were found quickly." River nodded toward Dempsey, who had returned. "Are we ready? It's not a super long walk out of the woods, but it is rather cold, and we've been outside for a while."

"This was *your* idea," Motts reiterated.

"I'm feeling harshly judged." River made his way out of the clearing with Motts following and Dempsey close behind her. "I've no idea how you found this little path. It's barely visible even with daylight."

"Lucky?"

"You found a serial killer's trophy shrine. I'd call that the polar opposite of lucky." Dempsey caught her arm when she tripped over a tree root. "Careful. Let's not get injured after you've been rescued."

CHAPTER FIFTEEN

"The elephant in the room" had always been a turn of phrase Motts found fascinating. The pachyderm lounging around the cosy fire in her parents' den happened to be where they'd all swanned off to at half-six in the morning. No one had asked.

Not directly.

A lot of pointed looks had been sent around.

Dempsey had thankfully chosen to stick with them. His presence had mollified her mum. And he'd likely also been the reason her normally nosy family had kept their peace about the morning's misadventure.

Granted, only five of them knew it had been a misadventure. So while everyone ate the sweet sticky buns her gran had made for breakfast and sipped coffee or tea, Motts had hugged her mug and tried to push away thoughts of the shrine in the woods.

Shining shrine sounds sordid soliloquies.

Not my best work.

Never is when everything stresses me out.

"Is no one going to explain where you all were this morning?" Her mum spoke up, forcing the issue after everyone had spent their entire breakfast not mentioning it. "The five of you head out, then return with a police escort."

"We went into Dulwich Woods for a walk." Her granddad was the one to respond when no one else seemed to know what to say. "Earlier than our usual, eh poppet?"

"Much earlier." Motts glared at her cousin, who beamed at her before shoving the last of his breakfast into his mouth. "I'll be in the garden. Cactus needs a break."

I need one as well.

Adjusting Cactus's cardigan, Motts grabbed a random coat from the rack by the front door and made her way through the house into the garden. It was too cold to be there for long. She just wanted a second to herself.

Her phone buzzed in her pocket. Motts found a

message from Dannel, hoping she'd fully recovered from her shutdown. She had to laugh, given the events of the morning.

Sitting in one of the garden chairs, Motts typed up a summarised version of what had happened while Cactus darted around. Osian quickly joined in their group chat, wanting all the details. The couple invited her to share the story on an upcoming podcast episode.

She sent them one of the videos of the shrine. They both agreed it was a disturbing find. They also thought she had quite possibly the worst luck.

Worse than theirs, and given the stories they'd shared, that was saying something.

"Is this where you hid as a child?" Dempsey sat in the seat beside hers, the one her dad usually took. Cactus immediately raced over to him. "In the garden?"

"Despite having the worst allergies to the flowers Mum insisted on planting, the garden was a safe haven for me." Motts finished up her message to Osian and Dannel, then put her phone away. "Why do you think the killer had the shrine near their old home?"

"Why do you think they did?" Dempsey turned the question around on her.

Motts had been thinking about it ever since they walked out of the woods. Why? Why had Hugo or Jonty or both returned to a place near their childhood home? Wouldn't it be a massive risk? How many people went down those paths every year? "Because it's where everything began. Here in Dulwich. It's the connection. Or maybe something happened in those woods or in that house? Something that triggered the start of the killing."

Dempsey nodded slowly. "We're trying to dig deeper into their past. It's been difficult to find people who remember their family. Hopefully, we'll find more answers as we comb through everything you found for us."

"You're welcome." Motts got to her feet and went to retrieve Cactus. "He's probably been out in the cold long enough."

"I should get back to the woods and see how they're doing." Dempsey followed her out the side gate. She figured he'd want to avoid a long goodbye with her nosy family. "I'll be heading to the hospital to check on Nathan Tellier as well. With any luck, he'll be conscious."

"Why do you think they've switched to teachers when it was initially all about the girls in my class?" Motts had assumed that if the killer wanted a "full set" of schoolgirls, it wouldn't have included any adults at her primary school. "Odd, isn't it?"

"I haven't decided how out of the ordinary it is. Not yet." Dempsey lingered by his vehicle. He patted Cactus on the head, chuckling when he stretched out for more. "If you could spend the rest of the holidays safe, sound, and quiet, it would do wonders for my blood pressure."

Turning back to the house after watching him, Motts found Vina waiting for her. She had a small wrapped box in her hands. Cactus was immediately interested in the bow.

"Sneaking presents early?"

"This one's for you." Vina waved the gift in front of her, yanking it away when Motts reached for it. "Beck sent you something."

"Beck?"

"I thought you weren't dating our local non-binary genius chef?" Vina exchanged the gift for Cactus.

"I got you a present. Are we dating?" Motts held a hand up when Vina went to respond. "Yes, I'm aware we used to go out together. I made Nish something as well. Christmas gifts do not a relationship make."

While Vina watched with as much curiosity as Cactus, Motts opened the present. She found a leather case inside. It was filled with custom-made quilling tools—all handcrafted with ergonomic grips.

"Oh." Motts gently ran her fingers along one of the grips. It was perfect. "I mentioned the quilling projects were taking longer than usual because my fingers had begun to hurt because of the slender tools."

"What were you saying about not dating?" Vina teased. She looped her arm around Motts's shoulders. "Why don't we sneak up to your room? You can give your new tools a try while River and Nish distract all the grown-ups."

"We're in our late thirties. Well, forty now." Motts kept forgetting she'd turned forty already. "I think we're the grown-ups."

"Does your mum think you're a grown-up?"

"Fair point."

CHAPTER SIXTEEN

CHRISTMAS DAY HAD DAWNED WITH THE USUAL nonsense from her family. River had woken her up early. They'd messed around in the kitchen with Gran and Granddad until everyone else in their family had gathered in the living room around the tree.

No holiday was complete without her mum's casual passive-aggressive comments about her choice of gifts. Motts had spent so much time carefully crafting the Christmas pudding ornaments. She'd even done an entire set just for herself. Still, she hadn't bothered to decorate the cottage since her holidays were being spent in Dulwich.

Her mum's narky comment about *rustic* gifts had been smoothed over by the rapturous praise from the rest of her family. Vina had even insisted on wearing hers like a brooch.

The rest of the present exchange had gone well, if a little muted, until her mum brought out a package for Motts. It had arrived the day before. No postage. No complete address. It had been left on the doorstep for her.

Motts gently lifted the package out of her mum's hands. "Nish? Vina? River? Could one of you run outside and grab DI Dorsey? I think he's the one outside. Have him call Dempsey?"

Gently carrying the box out into the garden, Motts placed it on one of the chairs. The temptation to open it was overwhelming. Curiosity poked at her common sense.

Deciding to distract herself, Motts snapped a photo of the box, then texted it over to Dempsey. He immediately responded, telling her to move as far away as possible and wait for them to show up. She decided he had a point and went into the house to find Detective Inspector Dorsey standing in the living room with his phone pressed to his ear.

"He's chatting with Dempsey." Vina stepped over to her. She leaned in to whisper. "They want us to evacuate the house. Your mum might actually faint."

"Why are we evacuating the house?" Motts

figured if the package had been some sort of explosive, it would've gone off already, given the rough handling the box had received. "We're a little late to be overly cautious."

They all eventually evacuated under the stoic glare of Detective Inspector Dorsey; her mum's arguments had been ignored. One of her parents' neighbours invited them into their house. Motts stayed outside with her group of friends.

The Explosive Ordnance Disposal Unit arrived quickly, considering it was Christmas. Motts was amused when River and Nish began trying to chat up Dorsey for information. However, she didn't think they were going to be successful.

"Oz and D think your luck is worse than theirs." Vina had been updating the group chat with the morning's events. "Think they're jealous."

"Ah, yes, so much to be jealous of." Motts gestured toward the multiple police vehicles blocking the street. "What if it's nothing?"

"Motts." Dempsey stepped out of her parents' house and waved at her. He led her through the house into the garden where the bomb squad was putting away their equipment. "It was safe to open. I thought you'd want to see what was inside."

"Beheaded origami cats." Motts peered into the

box. It was like someone had poured ice water down the back of her cardigan. She wrapped her arms around herself. "There are one hundred and ten."

"What?" Dempsey glanced sharply at her.

"I made these." Motts stumbled backwards and managed to find the empty chair behind her. "The commission came into my online shop four months ago. They wanted one hundred and ten origami cats."

"I'll need the customer's information, whatever you have on them." Dempsey crouched in front of her. He placed a hand on the arm of the chair. "Are you okay?"

"Fine."

"You don't seem fine." He sounded worried.

Or, Motts thought it was worry. She wasn't completely sure of the nuance in his voice. It could be concern, or it might also have been anger.

They sometimes felt the same. Motts watched one of the other detectives take the box of ruined origami and place it into a paper evidence bag. She had the irrational urge to laugh.

Is it irony to have folded paper in a paper bag?

"Motts?"

"My laptop is in my bedroom. I can access my Etsy seller account there. I can find at least a name, address, and email for you." Motts stood up and headed into the house, leaving him to follow her. "Why do this? Why send me a box of my own creations with their heads chopped off? What is the point aside from terrifying me?"

"That is the point. Fear." Dempsey followed her through the house into her bedroom. He had to stop to pick up Cactus, who'd darted between his legs a few times. "Are you trying to trip me up?"

Cactus simply butted his head against Dempsey's chin. Motts left them to converse while she dug her laptop from under a stack of papers on the bed. She shook her hands out a few times; her fingers wouldn't stop trembling, which made typing her password a tad difficult.

"Oh." Motts stared at the name listed on the order. She hadn't even considered it when she made and shipped the cats months ago. "Jenny B R Brow. Jenny Barbrow. They were… poking at the first death. Jenny's murder."

Dempsey placed a hand gently on her shoulder. "Can you write down the address?"

"It's a mailbox rental. I recognise the address." Motts took the notebook he offered to her then wrote down the name, address, and email as well.

"They've ordered from me once before. Two years ago."

"Why don't you forward me copies of both invoices?" Dempsey put his notebook away, then gently set Cactus down on the bed. "Why don't you stay up here for a bit? I imagine your family can clean up the wrapping paper in the living room without your help. The bomb squad has already gone. I'll be out of your hair as well. If anything else happens, anything at all, call me immediately. Promise?"

"I promise." Motts nodded. She clutched Cactus to her, carefully adjusting his cardigan. "I'm next, aren't I?"

"We're not going to allow anyone to come even close to hurting you." Dempsey gave her shoulder another squeeze, then stepped out of her room. He gently closed the door behind him.

Motts placed Cactus back on the bed. She grabbed her pillow, shoved her face into it, and let out a muffled scream. It didn't help. Much.

Meow. "Yes, Cactus, I'd like to go home as well. London's not been very welcoming this visit."

"Mottsy?" Vina queried quietly before knocking. "Can we come in?"

"Might as well." Motts discovered "we" meant

Vina, Nish, and River. The trio crept into her room, closing the door behind them. "Your mum wants to finish unwrapping presents."

"Of course she does." Motts fell back onto her bed with a groan. "Think anyone would notice if I just stayed up here for the rest of the day?"

"Probably." River sat on the floor, stretching his legs out in front of him. "What did they find in the box?"

"Beheaded origami cats." Motts wondered if it sounded as terrifyingly absurd to them as it did to her. "Over a hundred of them."

"Origami cats?" Nish joined River on the floor while Vina came over to sit on the edge of the bed. "Weren't you making loads of those in September or October?"

"I was. The very same ones they found in the box." Motts wasn't surprised when they all gasped. "I imagine he'll have more to tell later. They've taken the entire package with them. The address was a rental mailbox, though, and the name was definitely fake. Not sure what they'll discover."

"Mottsy." Vina shifted on the bed so she could grasp Motts's hand tightly. "Don't go anywhere without one of us. And your panic bracelet."

"I'm going to be fine." Motts didn't want any of

them to worry despite the trepidation taking an icy grip on her mind. "Perfectly fine."

"Perfectly fine?" Vina raised an eyebrow at her. "Perfectly. Fine. A serial killer sent you a box of decapitated cats."

"Paper ones." Motts felt the need to point out.

"Decapitated. Cats," Vina emphasised with a dramatic flair.

To Motts's surprise, they were left alone in her room for over an hour. Her dad finally poked his head inside and suggested they all come downstairs for lunch. A gentle request. He seemed a little shaken.

Motts frowned after him. "Did he seem odd?"

"Motts, my loveliest cousin, you do realise how terrifying it can be to see how much danger you are in? And not be able to do anything about it?" River pushed himself up off the floor, then reached down to help Nish up as well. "I imagine your dad is considering who left the package on your doorstep."

"Ah." Motts hadn't actually considered how any of this might be affecting those around her. She assumed they were all fine. "Are you worried?"

"Mildly," Vina answered.

"She means yes. Worried but choosing to be cautiously optimistic in the face of imminent doom."

River flopped dramatically on the bed between them.

"If you're going to narrowly cheat death, Detective Inspector Silver Fox is definitely who I'd choose to have with me." Vina fanned herself.

"You don't even like men," Nish pointed out helpfully.

"I can appreciate a thing of beauty even when it has the wrong bits and bobs." Vina grinned.

"Which are the bits and which are the bobs?" Motts shoved River off her and stood up. "We should get going. Mum won't be as polite as Dad."

The paper death kittens had definitely put a damper on Christmas Day. Motts hadn't explained much to the rest of the family. She didn't want to send her mother into another tirade.

She'd endured two already.

Motts didn't know if the package had everyone on edge or her mother's constant picking at everything. They were midway through the lovely lunch her gran, mother, and auntie had made when she snapped. "Please, please, please. Please stop saying things."

Every person around the table glanced in her direction. The attention was unbearable. She hated it.

Hated the tension.

Hated the insulting barbs her mother flung at her. "Wasting her time on her little paper nonsense." "I always knew you couldn't manage life alone." And the worst, "You're not clever enough to understand why living by yourself is dangerous." It left her seething with hurt and anger. Motts knew they were meant for her because everyone else ground their teeth in anger and kept glancing at her in concern. It was the opposite of a happy holiday.

"Poppet?" Her dad set his fork down. He'd been silent as always during lunch, content to allow the world to go on around him while he enjoyed his extra helping of Yorkshire pudding. "Are you okay?"

"I am going outside. For a walk. By myself." Motts stood up slowly, careful not to bump the table or knock her chair over. She held a hand up to stop Vina or Nish from getting up. Her granddad was frowning heavily at her mother. "I put my heart into making presents this year. I'm proud of them. Proud of my business that I started. Proud of how well I'm doing while living on my own in Cornwall. I'm sorry you don't feel the same, Mum."

Motts grabbed her coat from the rack by the door. She stalked out of the house and belatedly remembered Dempsey asking her not to go anywhere alone. *Does it count if the nice constable sitting in his car can see me?*

Probably not.

"Want some company?" Her auntie Lily stepped out of the house with a large shawl wrapped around her. "Walk."

Motts followed the order quickly. No one ignored her auntie. "Sorry."

"Why?" She narrowed her eyes at Motts. "You were correct. She was wrong."

"Okay."

"I was pleased when you moved to Cornwall. Closer to us. To River, who always missed you. You're more of a sister than a cousin, I think." She looped her arm around Motts's, leading her on a short circuit up and down the street. "You were a flower wilting in a hothouse here. Polperro has been good for your spirit."

CHAPTER SEVENTEEN

Boxing Day started with fewer dramatics. Motts had hidden away for the rest of Christmas with her headphones on, watching a Try channel playlist and avoiding everyone else in the house. She'd woken up early, had a long bath, then snuck back into her room to find her granddad had brought up a breakfast tray of food and mug of tea for her, complete with a handwritten note of encouragement.

Motts had folded it into a little crane, then set it on her nightstand. She shared some of her breakfast with Cactus. "We're going to have to leave the room eventually, I suppose."

"Morning, poppet." Her granddad took the tray from her, carrying it into the kitchen where her dad and uncle were making breakfast. A chaotic affair to say the least. "Your mother is upstairs with one of her headaches."

"Ah." Motts fidgeted uneasily.

"How about we send Cactus out into the garden where my Martha is enjoying her coffee? You and I can take an early morning walk. Pop by to see Janice Sallow, since I did tell her we'd be by." Her granddad plucked her cat off the floor and carried him out to the garden. "Who doesn't enjoy going visiting on Boxing Day?"

Me?

But Motts was curious to chat with her old teacher's caretaker. And she wouldn't be going alone if she went with her granddad. "Did you have breakfast already?"

"I did." He guided her out of the house after they'd said good morning to her gran and auntie, who were chatting in the garden. "If we're quick, we can get out before anyone tries to come with us."

The drive took no time at all. Motts didn't know if she was ready to engage in small talk with a total stranger. Her granddad, on the other hand, seemed more than prepared when he greeted Janice Sallow with a broad smile.

It was awkward. Motts barely managed a muted

hello. She definitely needed a few weeks in her cottage with no visitors to recover from her time in London.

Come home to London. It's safer in London. You'll be so much happier here. All things Motts's mum had told her in the past few days. London certainly didn't feel safer than Polperro.

"It's so lovely to meet you." Janice turned out to be a lovely woman in her fifties who'd been an in-home carer for the elderly for many years. "She always talked about all of her children. She had so many photos."

"Oh." Motts glanced uneasily around the room. It seemed quite empty compared to the brief view she'd gotten the day of the fire.

"I've moved most of the damaged furniture into the garden. Would you like to see it? Some of it came from her classroom," Janice offered when Motts kept staring out the sliding doors leading out back. "Go on. I'm sure your lovely granddad can keep me company."

Deciding to take the invitation to explore the garden, Motts left her granddad and Janice to chat. He'd get more out of her anyway. His charm tended to win over most people.

The garden wasn't anything special. Bog-standard. Motts remembered her conversation with Geoff Dixon about the man caught on video. She wandered along the perimeter of the fence on the off chance the police had missed something.

It was unlikely but better than staying inside the home that still smelled vaguely of fire and smoke. A desk sitting outside immediately drew her attention. She remembered one just like it at school.

Motts went over to check the desk out. She touched a finger over a gouge in the wood, one she recalled from one of their classmates dropping a bronze statue on it. *How'd she get her old desk? Did the school gift it? Why did she even want it? Happy memories?*

Does anyone have pleasant memories from school enough to want a desk?

There'd been rumours at school that Mrs Ceresto had a hidden compartment under her desk. Motts decided to answer the age-old question. She crouched down and managed to squeeze into the small space to investigate.

"Pineapple."

Motts jolted out from under the desk she'd been inspecting, bashing her head against the underside. "Ouch."

"You're Pineapple."

Motts stepped around the desk, putting it between herself and the fence Jonathan Barbrow was peering over. She rubbed her hands along her trousers and tried to slow down her suddenly racing heartbeat. "Jonty. I haven't seen you in ages."

Not officially, though I've a sneaking suspicion that you shoved me down a flight of stairs a few days ago.

"Haven't you?" He had a hoodie on with the hood up over his head, but she easily recognised him from the updated photos Dempsey had shown her. "He'll be angry if I ruin his fun."

"Oh?" Motts reached behind her, blindly scrambling for the shovel that had been leaning against the fence. She didn't know how effective it would be in allowing her to defend herself. It was better than nothing. "Who will be, Jonty? What sort of fun?"

Her bracelet dangled from her wrist. Motts was hesitant to press the button considering she'd already used it once. It felt excessive to do so again.

Was it crying wolf if the bad people really were after her?

"I imagine you'll find out eventually." Jonathan continued to scowl at her. The menace in his voice caused her to grip the shovel more tightly and hold it in front of her. "What are you doing here?"

"I was invited." Motts wanted to fling the question back in his face.

"Pineapple. Daft name."

I should press the panic button.

Should I press the panic button? Twice in a week seems a little excessive. Am I overreacting?

Can you overreact to a possible murderer standing in front of you?

"Thank you." Motts pressed the panic button. She had no doubts Dempsey would be wondering why she'd waited so long in the first place. "Why are you here?"

"Haven't you heard? Killers love to return to the scene of the crime." He grinned at her. Motts had never experienced such a menacing smile in her life. "I'd hoped the entire house would go up. Far less satisfying when all I've done is singe the furniture."

"I'm fairly certain Mrs Ceresto would feel differently." Motts took a step back from the desk when Jonathan slammed his hand against the top of the fence. He brought up his other arm, revealing a bottle. "You did plenty of damage."

"True enough. She deserved it." Jonathan slowly uncapped the bottle. His gaze almost seemed to be going right through her. It was unnerving.

"Oi. What are you doing over there?" Geoff

Dixon stepped out of his house into his garden. "You're on camera. I've called the police."

With a strangled cry of frustration, Jonathan flung the bottle at her. It hit the desk, sending liquid flying across the wooden surface. Motts jumped out of the way, stumbling over a partially burnt chair and tumbling to the ground.

Motts scrambled to her feet, surprised to find the shovel somehow still in her hand. She clutched it to her body. "What an absolute berk."

Berk?

Yes, let's call the potential serial killer a berk. Like all he's done is stolen my lunch from me.

Maybe something stronger?

"He's gone." Geoff came over to his side of the fence. "I've got him on camera. Mind the desk; fairly certain he's flung some sort of acid at you."

Motts was stunned to find a corrosive liquid bubbling away on top of the wood. She ran her hands over her coat, checking to make sure none had splashed onto her. "Well, that is terrifying."

Terrifyingly torturous toxic twists.

The police arrived relatively quickly. They'd asked her to remain outside while her granddad and Janice remained in the house. She'd suggested that

Detective Inspector Dorsey ask Geoff Dixon for his CCTV footage.

"I believe this would be the point in most shows on the telly where I tell you that 'we have to stop meeting like this.'" Dempsey joined Motts in the garden. He'd been the last to arrive; he was dressed more casually than she'd ever seen him. She particularly liked the ugly Christmas sweater. "Are you all right?"

Motts nodded shakily. She drew her coat more tightly around her. "None of the acid hit me. I assume it's acid from the way it's eating slowly into the desk."

"Did he say anything?"

"Admitted to killing Mrs Ceresto without saying the actual words. London is exhausting." Motts wanted to sit down, but she was afraid to touch anything. She couldn't stop staring at the bubbling liquid on the desk. "Think I'll go back to Cornwall early."

"Why don't we get you inside?" Dempsey suggested.

"You sound worried." Motts glanced up when he sighed. "What?"

Leading her into the house, Dempsey asked her granddad and Janice to step into another room. He wanted one of his detectives to speak with them separately. Motts waved weakly at her granddad when he paused to check on her before leaving the kitchen.

"Are you making tea in someone else's kitchen?" Motts watched him fill an electric kettle and switch it on. He grabbed a chair from the nearby table and carried it over for her. "I…."

"Why don't you have a seat and give yourself a moment?" Dempsey dug around in the cupboards before finding a tin of shortbread. He pried the lid off and offered her one. "Eat. You're experiencing shock. The adrenaline from coming face-to-face with Jonty is crashing. I imagine you'd prefer to avoid another hospital visit."

"I would." Motts nibbled on the shortbread. Did it even have enough sugar to affect her? "Jonty said hurting me would ruin 'his' fun. And he wasn't referring to himself."

"He who?"

"At a guess? Hugo?" Motts took an even smaller bite when her stomach churned uneasily. "What if one brother kills former students and the other has decided to go after the teachers?"

"You'd make a brilliant detective."

"I'd make a terrible detective." Motts watched

him drop an obscene number of sugar cubes into her cup. "Are you trying to make me ill?"

"Sugar's good for shock."

"I'm not shocked."

"Feeling a little shaky?" Dempsey raised an eyebrow when she shrugged. He finished making her tea, then placed the mug in front of her. "You are. Your hands are trembling, and I imagine it's not from the cold. Drink your tea, then we'll talk."

CHAPTER EIGHTEEN

An hour of rehashing what had happened with Jonty had Motts more than ready to leave. She appreciated Dempsey's gentle approach. It had just been a lot.

On the drive back to her parents', Motts mulled over what Jonathan Barbrow had said. She didn't know if he'd been the one to attack Mrs Ceresto. It seemed like he had, but she was convinced Hugo was Jenny's killer.

It was, at the moment, impossible to prove.

"There you are, darling." Her mother accosted her the second she arrived home. Motts closed her eyes and hoped for patience. Her granddad stayed with her in the entryway; she hadn't even gotten fully into the house. "Your father and I believe you must move back to Dulwich. It's safer here."

"Safer? In London? When I've been shoved down a flight of stairs and had acid thrown at me? How is this better than Cornwall?" Motts tried to get by her mother, who blocked the hallway. "Why do you find it so difficult to believe I've found happiness in Polperro?"

"You're ruining your life."

"How?" Motts bent down to pluck Cactus off the rug when he pawed at her leg repeatedly. "How precisely am I ruining my life? My business has grown significantly since I moved to Polperro. My bouquets are in several bridal shops. I've sold more of my quilling artwork than ever before. You should be proud of me. I'm living independently. Successfully. What's the real truth, Mum? Have I ruined your vision of what my life would be?"

"Poppet? Why don't you take your little man upstairs? I'm sure he's ready for his mid-morning nap." Her granddad rested a hand on her shoulders and gently pushed her past her mother. "I've a few things to say to Rose, here."

Briefly glancing between her granddad and mother, Motts flew upstairs to her childhood bedroom. It evoked the oddest sense of déjà vu for her, of so many moments from her teenage years. Especially when she'd hidden away to avoid the constant weight of crushing disappointment.

The difference, Motts supposed, was now she had control over her life. She didn't have to remain in Dulwich. Not for a second longer than she wanted.

Grabbing her phone, Motts scrolled down to find the group chat. She sent a message to see if any of them were ready to return to Polperro. It was a long enough drive; she didn't fancy making it on her own.

Also, she didn't have a car.

Vina responded to the chat first; not a surprise. She'd seen Taara off at the airport that morning and was more than ready to head home. Motts asked for a pickup; she wanted to pop by the hospital to see Mr Tellier before leaving Dulwich.

If her teacher was awake, Motts wanted to see if Jonathan had said anything before the attack. She probably should leave it to Dempsey. It was impossible to let go, though; she'd been drawn into it by the killers themselves.

"Can I come in, poppet?" Her dad knocked twice. "Poppet?"

"It's open." Motts tossed her phone on the bed,

then went to grab her bag. She wanted to begin packing her things up. "Did Mum send you up?"

"No, your granddad did." He hesitated before stepping fully into the room. "You're leaving?"

"I...." Motts had never been able to get her father to understand how much stress and anxiety being around her mother caused. "Vina wanted to head back early, and she's my ride. Riding rider rides riddles."

A little white lie never hurt anyone, did it?

"We love you, poppet. I hope you know that we love you very much." He had his hands in the pockets of his cardigan. "You're welcome to stay through the New Year."

"I know, Dad." She smiled weakly but continued to fold up the clothes she'd taken out of her bag. Cactus tried to climb inside and curl up on them. "Is this your idea of helping?"

Meow.

"Maybe be less helpful?" Motts lifted him out of the bag and placed him on her pillow instead. She peered back at her dad, still hovering by the door. "Mum is never going to understand my life. Or appreciate it. She probably thinks if she finds just the right diet, maybe I'll be normal enough to lead a life she can be proud of."

"We are proud of you, poppet."

Are you?

Motts shrugged. She didn't have the energy to engage in the same argument over and over with them. "I've had a lovely Christmas, Dad. I love you very much."

He came over to give her a hug, kissing the top of her head. "I've always been proud of you."

Watching him leave the room, Motts wished he'd been more vocal in his support. Instead, she shook her head and sighed. Polperro and her warm cottage had never seemed quite so welcoming.

She was ready to go home.

The cliffs, the sea, the village all beckoned to her.

Meow.

"Yes, we are going home. I'm sure everyone will be thrilled to bask in your presence." Motts deftly caught Cactus before he snuck into her bag for a second time. "We've got to wait for Vina to come and pick us up. No, you're not riding in my backpack."

In no time at all, Motts had her clothes and presents packed up. She'd remained in her room undisturbed. A door down the hall had slammed ten minutes after her dad left her alone; her mother was probably fed up from being told off by her granddad.

Her grandparents had never been shy about intervening on her behalf.

Vina: Are you ready? Want me to come in?

Motts: Just a second, saying goodbye to everyone.

Vina: You sure you don't want me to come inside? I know how your mum can be.

Motts: She's in her room with a migraine. Just dad and the grandparents. Gran's packing up food for us.

Vina: Yes. Get in. Gran Mottley snacks are delish.

Motts: You've been watching too much telly again, haven't you? 'Get in.'

Vina: Don't judge. I'm trying to stay young.

The goodbyes weren't quite as painful as Motts feared. She made it outside without too much fuss. Her gran had already packed up a little picnic basket of treats for them.

"You ready?" Vina stood outside her vehicle with the boot open. She grabbed Motts's backpack and then motioned to place the picnic hamper and Cactus's carrier into the back seat. "Should you warn the poor constable who's been trying to keep up with you all week?"

"I messaged Dempsey. Told him we'd be going home." Motts hesitated after getting Cactus secured in the back seat. "Do you mind if we swing by the hospital? I wanted to see if Mr Tellier is awake."

"Do you now?"

"Vina." Motts narrowed her eyes when Vina continued to tease her. "Aren't you the least bit curious about if he heard anything when he was attacked?"

"Of course. Maybe we don't tell DI Silver Fox this part." Vina motioned for her to get into the vehicle. "Maybe we should let the constable know we're leaving? I doubt they want to follow us all the way to Cornwall. Bit of a long jaunt for a London constable to make."

They had a brief conversation with the constable, who wished them a safe journey. He'd apparently be watching her parents' house for a few days more. Motts didn't think the Barbrows would visit with her leaving.

Why bother?

They'd avoided any sort of collateral damage

throughout their career as killers. Hugo, at least, had a definite single-mindedness to him. An almost strict adherence to who he intended to murder.

On the way to the hospital, Motts gave Vina a brief recap of her morning. It had been an eventful Boxing Day, between the literal acid from Jonathan and the figurative acid from her mother. However, she smiled genuinely for the first time when Vina promised a detour to Portsmouth for a night before continuing on to Polperro; they already had a room booked.

"Hello, Motts. Fancy meeting you here."

Motts stopped just inside the hospital lobby when Detective Inspector Dorsey walked towards her. "Hello."

"Visiting someone?"

"I'm going home to Cornwall today, but I wanted to pop by to see Mr Tellier if he's awake." Motts thought it sounded plausible. People went to visit others in the hospital. "Do you know if he is?"

"He is. How about I escort you to the room so the staff don't give you any trouble?" Dorsey gave her a jaunty wink, then waved at her to follow him. "Run into any further trouble?"

"Not really. Were you here to question him?" Motts had seen DI Dorsey at Mrs Ceresto's house.

"The chief wants to be the one to talk with him. I'm here to make sure no one tries to finish the job." Dorsey lowered his voice when they went by a nurses' station. "They don't seem the sort to give up when a first attempt fails, do they?"

"No." Motts shuddered, thinking about the acid bubbling on the desk. It was the image she couldn't get out of her mind. "They don't."

"In you go. I'll wait outside. Let you have a moment on your own." He opened the door for her with a smile. "Try not to ask probing questions, would you?"

With a shy smile, Motts nodded, then stepped into the room. She tried not to cringe at the distinct smell of hospital cleaning supplies. It made her nose burn.

"Pineapple." Mr Tellier spotted her creeping quietly into the room. "No need to tiptoe. I'm awake and mostly in control of my faculties."

"How are you?" Motts thought he seemed more alert than she'd expected, given the massive amount of bruising on him. "Were you badly hurt?"

"I'd say I'd had worse—but I haven't." He winced while attempting to adjust the pillow behind him. "Though I'm alive, so I'm lucky."

"Do you remember anything from the attack?"

"Vaguely. It was definitely a bald man. Thought it was Jonathan Barbrow, but maybe my head's too addled from being knocked about." He closed his eyes for a few seconds. "The thing I recall most clearly is him whispering, 'That's number two for me.' He was talking to himself, not to me. Everything else is a blur."

"That's number two for me?"

Had Jonty meant two murders? Maybe he'd wrongly assumed Mr Tellier was dead, and that made two deaths to his name. Are they competing with each other?

Before Motts could ask another question, there was a scuffle outside the room. She heard DI Dorsey shouting at someone. Mr Tellier glanced over in alarm.

"Press the emergency call button," Motts ordered. She had her finger on her bracelet while inching toward the door and slowly opening it to find the detective gone. "What the—"

Staring down the hall, Motts noticed a door to a stairwell open. She raced towards it and heard fighting several flights down. DI Dorsey was on the ground with blood coming from a cut above his eyebrow by the time she got to him.

No one else in sight.

Motts knelt down beside him. She placed her

fingers on his neck to feel for a pulse. *Strong beat.* "Detective Inspector? Can you hear me?"

A muffled moan was the only response. Motts heard footsteps below and immediately got to her feet. She had no idea how to defend herself without a weapon; thankfully, it was hospital security coming clattering up the stairs towards them.

"He needs help," Motts stated the obvious, returning to kneel beside DI Dorsey. "Someone attacked him."

"Someone?"

Motts wilted at the glower coming from the very tall, incredibly intimidating security officer. "Well, it certainly wasn't me. I came on the scene after."

I came on the scene.

I've been chatting with too many police officers lately.

"We'll see about that." He motioned for Motts to move away from the detective inspector. "Why don't you stand over there until we sort all of this out?"

CHAPTER NINETEEN

Sorting it out took longer than Motts anticipated. The security officer finally stopped staring suspiciously at her when DI Dorsey woke up. He was able to identify his attacker as Jonathan Barbrow.

Definitely a man.

Definitely not Motts.

The security officer released her. Motts made her way out of the hospital to where Vina had been impatiently waiting for her. She ran into Dempsey in the lobby; he barely managed to stop from colliding with her.

"Motts?"

"Hello." She waved uncomfortably, not knowing what DI Dorsey had told him. "I'm heading home."

"So you mentioned in your text message earlier. You appear to have made a detour to the hospital." Dempsey caught her by the arm to pull her out of the walkway leading up to the entrance. "Dorsey didn't mention you were visiting Tellier."

"I heard shouting. I found DI Dorsey at the bottom of the stairs."

"Of course you did." Dempsey massaged his forehead briefly then gave a wry chuckle. "Can you at least attempt to stay out of trouble on the drive to Cornwall?"

"I'll do my best." Motts patted him on the arm gently. "There, there, I'm sure it's all going to be okay."

Saying goodbye, Motts quickly found Vina with Cactus curled up in her arms. They'd both obviously grown tired of waiting. It took a moment to get settled before they were on their way out of Dulwich.

They lucked out with traffic, maybe because of the day. They managed to arrive in Portsmouth in under two hours. Their hotel was lovely, with a great view of the port.

"I'm chuffed. This was a brilliant idea." Vina sat on the edge of one of the double beds. She had a pizza box beside her. They'd had two delivered to their rooms, opting to relax after an exhausting stay in London. "And if we leave early enough, we can be home by lunchtime. My parents are thrilled. They're fixing a feast for us."

They'd decided to stay in Portsmouth for a full day and head to Polperro on the twenty-eighth. It was nice to hang out in a comfortable hotel room, watch YouTube videos, and relax for the first time in weeks.

"A Griffin feast means some sort of curry. I can't wait." Motts grabbed a slice of pizza and took a bite. She shifted the box out of Cactus's reach. "Not cat approved."

"I think you've offended him, poor beast." Vina laughed when Cactus slunk up to disappear underneath one of the pillows. "Any news from DI Silver Fox?"

"I wish you'd stop calling him DI Silver Fox. One of these days, I'm going to say it to his face, then I will have to die of mortification. No choice. Just die of embarrassment." Motts grabbed her phone to double-check before shaking her head. "Not even a single text message. I'm assuming they haven't caught Jonty. Surely Dempsey would've told me, right? So I can stop worrying."

"No point in worrying about any of it now,

Mottsy. We're well out of Dulwich." Vina leaned back against the pillows on her bed. "Safe from your mum and from serial-killing numpties."

"Serial-killing numpties. If we ever have our own podcast, that's what we're calling it." Motts grinned at Vina, who immediately started to laugh. "Can you imagine?"

"We could—"

"I was only joking. I do not have the mental energy to spare for a podcast. Did you see how much work Osian and Dannel put into theirs?" Motts grabbed her phone, deciding to send the couple an update on what had happened on her last day in the city. It would make an interesting addition to the episode they planned to record on the Dulwich schoolgirl killings. "Pretty sure I don't need any extra attention when it comes to murder."

"Still a good name for it. Serial-Killing Numpties." Vina snickered. "Maybe we can convince Nish and River to do it?"

"You just want to call them numpties."

"Fair point." Vina didn't seem at all repentant. "You could always text DI Silver Fox. Ask him if they've found Jonty?"

Ignoring Vina's request, Motts grabbed her laptop out of her backpack and set it up. She found a live stream from one of their favourite channels and pressed play. They both settled down to enjoy pizza and the video.

Motts got halfway through her second slice of pizza before her phone rang. She scowled at it but finally checked to find the caller was Dempsey. "Hello?"

"Where are you?" He sounded out of breath.

Motts ignored Vina's trying to grab her attention. Instead, she set her pizza to one side. "We've stopped for the night in Portsmouth. Why?"

"DNA results are finally in from the Ceresto case." Dempsey paused to shout something away from his phone. "Sorry. We're a little chaotic here. But we've got enough evidence now to get an arrest warrant signed off for Jonathan Barbrow."

"His DNA was at the scene?"

"I obviously cannot divulge any information to a member of the public." Dempsey waited for several seconds before continuing. "We haven't been able to find either brother in the city. Our most recent CCTV footage shows one of them leaving Dulwich in a pale blue Nissan. The vehicle was found two hours ago abandoned off the A3 near Petersfield. No cameras in the area. We can only assume they've stolen another car. No reports thus far."

"Petersfield? Off the A3?" Motts had a vague recollection of driving by the town on their way to Portsmouth. "You think they're following us."

"I have no reason to believe you're in danger."

"But no reason to believe we aren't in danger either?" Motts knew it could be either side of the coin. She preferred to err on the side of being overly cautious. "We'll leave in the morning for Polperro."

"I've reached out to the local police in Polperro. They've promised me they'll keep an eye out." Dempsey still sounded slightly out of breath.

"Are you running?"

"We've got a lot going on at the moment," he responded without giving her an answer. "Just be careful. Don't hesitate to hit your panic button or call 999 if anything seems out of the ordinary."

"I'll be careful. Promise." Motts hung up after he'd said his goodbyes. She glanced over to find Vina packing up her clothes. "We're not leaving in the middle of the night."

"True, but there's nothing wrong with being prepared." Vina continued rearranging everything in her bag. "Why don't we sneak out early in the morning? We can beat traffic."

"Traffic on a Saturday?" Motts picked at the crust on her pizza. Dempsey's call had increased her anxiety. She couldn't blame Vina for wanting to get on the road early, hopefully, make it home without a run-in with the Barbrows. "How early are we talking?"

"We'll set the alarm for six and see how things go." Vina put her box of pizza in the fridge. "We can have the rest in the morning for breakfast."

Neither of them slept that night despite their best efforts. Motts tried every trick she knew, but nothing helped. Her mind refused to shut off. All she could think about was the fire at Mrs Ceresto's house and the Barbrows being after her.

At half-past five, they both decided to give up. What was the point in lounging in bed and staring up at the ceiling? They managed to get packed up and on the road before six, record time for Vina, especially.

Cold pizza and bottled water got them through the first couple of hours of their journey. By the time they skirted by Exeter, Motts and Vina were both ready for a cup of tea. They pulled off at the next services exit, ready to stretch their legs and have something other than leftovers.

They managed to get bacon and cheese toasties and tea at the Costa drive-thru. Motts dug into the basket her gran had sent with them to find a few leftover sweet treats as well. There was even a treat for Cactus.

Gran always thought of everything. The last leg of their almost four-hour journey went fairly quickly. They drove through Looe, and Motts couldn't resist a quick stop by one of her favourite beaches despite Vina wanting to hurry home.

Leaving Vina and Cactus in the safety of the vehicle, Motts trudged down the path to the beach. She ignored the drizzling rain and the wind slamming into her. The sound of the waves against the shore settled her mind more than anything else had since she'd left for London a few weeks ago.

The sea had always had a calming effect on her. Motts walked along the shore and breathed in the Cornish air. Home. She wanted to wrap the ocean, wind, and wildness around her like a blanket.

Allow it to shield her from all the manic chaos in her life.

There was a blissful silence in the roaring of the waves. Motts allowed it to sink into her. Despite the cold, rain, and wind, she stayed on the sand until her shoulders began to lower and stress seeped out of her.

Motts found herself smiling. She tilted her head

to stare up at the grey skies and allowed the rain to pelt her face. "Thanks for the welcome home."

Chuckling to herself, Motts made her way back to the car park. She slipped into the vehicle, grateful to return to the heat. Vina raised an eyebrow at her then handed over a napkin from the picnic basket.

"Finished communing with the sea?" Vina waited until she nodded before driving up the lane away from the beach. "Lovely, isn't it? To be home again."

"Do you ever wish you lived in London?" Motts had never settled in Dulwich even as a child. Cornwall had been where she preferred to be. Something her mother had always hated. Her mother had wanted to get as far away from her childhood home as possible, the rare thing they had in common. "Somewhere livelier?"

"I have at times. I love our little village. Being close to my parents. I travel to London more than anyone else, but I'm always happy to be home." Vina shrugged. She eased the car along the narrow lanes. "I imagine you'd be happy to never have to leave Cornwall ever again."

"I'd definitely rather be here than anywhere else." Motts winced at all the sand on the floorboard. "I owe you a good hoovering of your car."

"No worries. Dad loves detailing the car. He'll be

over the moon to get his mini Hoover out. Strange man." Vina laughed loudly, which made Cactus meow in response. "We got him a whole kit for Christmas last year."

"Odd."

"Parents." Vina shrugged.

Begging off lunch with the Griffins, Motts asked to be dropped off at her home. She wanted some time in her cottage. Vina insisted on stopping by the Salty Seaman, their local fish and chip shop, to grab her something to eat.

Motts was finally alone in her cottage after what felt like months and months. She released Cactus from his carrier and simply stood in her living room. "Well, we made it."

CHAPTER TWENTY

After carrying her bag to her bedroom, Motts returned to find Cactus had ensconced himself on the cushion by the window looking out into the garden. She smiled at the familiar image, then went to get a fire going. Unfortunately, the weather had taken a turn for the worse.

A winter storm had begun to blow through. Wind, icy rain, and more wind. Motts found her thickest socks and a comfortable cardigan. She grabbed her lunch and sat in the armchair by the fireplace to eat.

"Nice to be home, isn't it?" Motts smiled when Cactus crept over to her. He made himself comfortable on the arm of her chair. "Wanting fish?"

Meow.

The silence in her cottage had never seemed more welcoming. Motts intended to enjoy every second of it. The wind howled outside, but they stayed comfortable ensconced under blankets by the fire, catching up on Vlogmas videos she'd missed from her favourite YouTube channels.

Tired of sitting after the first video wrapped up, Motts decided to get to work. She had to reopen her online shop and prepare to post a few items. Despite the wind and ice, she wanted to get out into the garden and check on everything.

After someone had destroyed her garden by throwing a caustic chemical over the fence, Motts had been forced to dig everything up. Her granddad and Hughie Stone, their local constable, had helped her clear the garden and build raised boxes. They hadn't managed to get anything planted, though.

At some point, Motts hoped to clear out her tiny greenhouse shed. It would allow her to get some seedlings planted for spring. She hoped for a fresh start with an excellent crop of vegetables and herbs, one that wouldn't be destroyed by a murderer out to frighten her.

Making her way into the kitchen, Motts made a list of everything she needed from the market. She'd emptied out her fridge and cupboards before heading to London. Hopefully, the storm wouldn't put her off running down to the village to get a few necessities.

With her list made, Motts grabbed her coat to head out into the garden. Everything appeared to be okay. She shivered against the wind but enjoyed the sound of the icy rain pelting her roof. Musical. Almost magical given the time of year.

The cameras installed on the cottage also appeared to be fine. No one had messed with them. They reminded her to message Teo to see how his Christmas had been.

Since he'd moved to Yorkshire along with his parents and grandmother, Motts had only seen the detective inspector a few times. However, she did miss him and was glad they'd been able to maintain their friendship after their dating life had fizzled out. *I should pick up the post; I wonder if Doc and Elys opened the post office today.*

"Be sure not to let any strangers into the cottage." Motts gave Cactus a quick scratch. She made sure he had water and food. "Yes, I'll pick up treats for you."

She'd have to wait for her full grocery list when Vina was free to drive with her to one of the nearby supermarkets. For now, she'd make do with the local shop that provided enough to get her by for the next few days. Life in a small village did have the occasional drawback.

Motts stepped outside and almost fell back against the door. Perhaps not the best day to walk down to the village. She was glad they'd arrived when they had. Driving in this sort of weather would've been stressful. "Well… no point in waiting. Milk won't buy itself."

Gingerly taking the stairs leading down into the village, Motts slipped once on the slippery steps. She caught herself on the railing. *Right, not my absolute best idea, but we're already halfway there, so what's the point in stopping now?*

"Bit of a gale out there, isn't it?" Doc greeted her when she stepped into the post office. "How was London then? Did you see the queen?"

"Yes. Okay. No." Motts answered his questions succinctly, which made the older man chuckle. "Did you have a lovely Christmas?"

"I did. I could've brought up your post when the weather isn't trying to blow us all around." Doc disappeared in the back then returned with a small satchel full of mail. "You've got loads of cards and one package from Yorkshire."

"A package?" Motts hadn't expected to receive anything from Teo, who was the only person she knew up in Yorkshire. "Thanks for holding my mail for me."

"Anytime, duckie." Doc helped her stow everything away in her backpack. "Are you sure you can manage the walk up the stairs in this weather? Don't go tumbling down. The steps might be slick."

"I won't take a second tumble. I'll be fine." Motts waved her thanks, then headed out the door before Doc or his lovely wife could offer any suggestions to her. The wind and ice hit her in the face again the moment she stepped outside. "Bugger."

By the time Motts had picked up a few things at the shop, she'd begun to resemble a frozen and bedraggled dog. So she made a detour to Griffin Brews. A hot chai latte and something fresh from the oven sounded brilliant.

"Well, hello," Cadan greeted her from behind the counter. "Fancied a walk in the storm?"

"I was out of milk." Motts hefted up her backpack, where she'd stored everything. "Have any pasties?"

"You're in luck. We made shepherd's pie ones today with just a hint of spice." Cadan grabbed one of the paper sacks and placed a few pasties and a sticky bun into it. "Chai latte as well?"

Motts nodded. "Did you have a good week?"

"A quiet one. Never the same when our twins are away." Cadan grabbed one of their reusable cups and filled it for her. "Our Vina can give you a ride home. Not sure the weather's going to calm down in the next few minutes."

"I'll be fine."

When Motts once again stood outside in the icy rain, she slightly regretted her decision. She trudged through the village, pausing to say a quick hello to Hughie when he drove past in his police vehicle. The trip up the stairs was even more treacherous than the way down had been.

Returning to her cottage, Motts was part popsicle when she finally got inside. She carried her backpack into the house with Cactus following close behind. He closely inspected the bag when she set it down on the kitchen table.

"Guess who sent us a package?" Motts put the cold stuff away in the refrigerator then grabbed her post from the bottom of her backpack. "One of your favourite detective inspectors."

The box, though compact, was surprisingly heavy. Motts grabbed scissors to cut through the tape. She chuckled when she found the package filled with chocolate bars.

Her weakness.

On the top of the bars was a new knitted cardigan for Cactus, along with a toy filled with catnip. The latter was immediately grabbed out of her hand. Her cat raced off with it, rolling around on the rug in front of the fire.

"That's you sorted for the rest of the day." Motts picked through the chocolate bounty in the package. She settled on a white chocolate raspberry mousse bar. "Nothing wrong with dessert first, right?"

Grabbing her chocolate bar, one of the pasties, and her latte, Motts settled into her favourite armchair and dragged a blanket across her lap. She sent a message to Teo, thanking him for the present. It was a lovely surprise.

Teo: Weren't you staying in London until after New Year's?

Motts: Parental pressure led to a change of plans. Did you get the package I sent you?

Teo: I meant to text you today. I just opened it. Thank you. I'll be taking him to my office—what better place for your masterful paper art of Saint Michael?

Motts: Patron saint of the police.

Teo: So he is. How are you doing? DCI

**Byrne told me about the recent develop-
ments in his case.**

Motts: Fine.

Teo: Fine?

Motts: Fine figures finally fine.

Teo: So fine.

Motts: Cactus loves his cardigan.

**Teo: Good. Motts. Please make sure to
take care of yourself. It's okay to admit
you're worried or frightened. To ask for
help. And it's okay to set boundaries even
when it comes to family.**

Teo was right. Motts still didn't know how to
process everything from her visit to Dulwich. She
distracted herself by skimming through the footage
from her security cameras; she'd only checked them
briefly throughout her time away from the cottage.

What if she'd missed something?

They knew for certain Jonathan Barbrow had
been in and around London through much of
December. Hugo was a different story. Was he with
his brother? Had he left the country again?

The Barbrows seemed remarkably talented at

escaping undetected. Travelling unnoticed. Motts didn't know what to think.

An hour of the most boring video in the world offered her no insight. Nothing out of the ordinary appeared to have happened around her cottage in her absence. A relief. She set her laptop aside and settled further into her chair.

Motts smiled when Cactus abandoned his new toy to curl up in her lap. "Nice to be home, isn't it?"

Meow.

"Yes, Teo did do a nice job on your new cardigan. It'll keep you warm." Motts ran her fingers along the knitted fabric. She couldn't help glancing over at her laptop, where the live feed from the garden camera continued to stream on the screen. "We're going to be okay, Cactus."

CHAPTER TWENTY-ONE

"You know what we need, Cactus? Routine." Motts had woken up to find the storm had blown over. Literally and figuratively. Her garden looked more windswept than usual. A part of her shed's roof now rested against the fence. "Brilliant. That's my day sorted."

Getting out of bed and wrapping herself up in a robe, Motts wandered downstairs to find breakfast, detouring into the living room to get the fire going to chase away the chill. Cactus immediately made himself comfortable on her armchair.

Motts got to her feet once the fire was roaring away. She tucked her hands into her robe, pausing to take in her cosy cottage. So different from her parents' house. "Chocolate for breakfast?"

Cactus chose to simply stare at her.

"Is that a yes or a no?" Motts stretched slowly, trying to avoid her muscles tightening up. Her periodic night sweats meant sleep was often not as restful as she'd like. Getting old was exhausting.

Breakfast wound up being a strong mug of tea along with one of the pasties Cadan had sent her home with. She warmed it up in her microwave, then set out Cactus's breakfast. They both needed a return to their regular schedule.

Cactus had a brief walk in the garden before Motts shuffled him back into the warmth of the cottage. Even with his cardigan, he didn't do so well in the cold. She returned outside to begin cleaning up the mess left by the storm.

"Anyone home?"

"You can see me, Hughie." Motts glanced over to find the tall, bear-like constable peering over the garden gate. "Literally."

"So, yes?" Hughie grinned broadly at her. "I wanted to check in to see if you had any damage from the storm."

"A little to the fence and my shed. One of the cameras at the front of the cottage was blown off. No idea where it ended up." Motts had searched around her home and along the coastal path that ran to the right of her garden fence. "How about the village?"

"A few things knocked over here and there. We were lucky." Hughie rested his arms on top of the fence. "Want some help cleaning up?"

"I'm almost done, to be honest." Motts had gathered up the damaged wood and dumped it in one corner of her garden. Her granddad might have a use for it. "Not sure how I'm going to fix the shed roof."

Her shed was half greenhouse and half storage. Her granddad and Hughie had helped her put it together. She hoped one of them had an idea for fixing both it and her fence.

"How about I grab my tools from home and other supplies? I can swing by later this afternoon to patch up the roof and fence. Won't take long," Hughie offered immediately.

When tourists and traffic in their village slowed down to almost nothing during the off-season, Hughie played handyman around Polperro. He'd been a great help when she first moved into the cottage. It had been fortuitous, since he'd been the one to find the skeleton buried in the corner of her garden.

She still wondered if she should've taken that first mystery as an omen. *Cornwall: here lies dead bodies. Buyer beware.* "That'd be lovely, thank you. I might pop into the village for lunch."

"I can come by after three? I've got a few more villagers to check on." Hughie waved jauntily, then disappeared out of view.

"Bye, Hughie." Motts returned her attention to the last of the raised beds. She'd cleared all the debris blown into her garden by the storms. But, given the strength of the wind, it surprised her nothing else had been damaged.

When Motts returned to the cottage, she found Cactus sitting by her phone. She'd left it on the coffee table. A green light flashed periodically, and Cactus tried to paw at it.

"Did someone message me?" Motts saved her phone from Cactus's attempts to send it flying off the coffee table. Instead, she found a text from Dempsey asking her to call. "Why am I suddenly filled with a sense of dread?"

Cactus didn't have an answer for her. Motts wandered into the kitchen and made a cup of tea. She found the nerve to call him when she'd finished drinking it.

"Motts?"

"What's happened?" Motts didn't bother with hello. He hadn't.

"I'm on my way to Cornwall."

"Driving while talking is dangerous."

"I'm not the one driving," Dempsey responded quickly. "Dorsey's with me. We caught Hugo Barbrow on camera re-entering the country on a ferry from Calais."

"Coming from where?"

"We're not sure where he was before Calais. I'm working with the French authorities and Interpol to track him. Hold on." Dempsey went silent, obviously having muted the call. Motts used the time to check her front door. Locked. She wandered around double-checking all of the windows. "Still there?"

"Where would I have gone? Never mind." Motts realised a second too late it was a rhetorical question. She focused instead on something that was bothering her. "Why are you heading to Cornwall if he just returned on a ferry? Wouldn't he be in London?"

"The footage from the port is days old."

"Days?" Motts returned to the front door to triple check the lock. "Days."

"I can't say for certain he's with Jonathan, who I do know for certain has headed south from London." Dempsey paused to speak with DI Dorsey for a second time. "We know one thing about Hugo

Barbrow. He is meticulously making his way through your classmates. And has done for over thirty years. You are the only living person in England that could be on his list."

"Dempsey." Motts resisted the urge to check all the locks again. "You don't—"

"I've dedicated much of my career to tracking killers and solving cold cases. These types of murderers. The desire doesn't go away if they're thwarted by circumstances." Dempsey cut her off ruthlessly. "You *are* in danger. And I'd rather be close by until we've caught the bastards."

"I'll be fine."

"Keep your doors locked. Try to avoid going on walks by yourself. Stick to the village for now. Please?" Dempsey urged. "For the sake of my sanity, if nothing else? Oh, I have to go, another call coming in. I'll be in touch."

Motts frowned down at her phone when the call ended without her being able to say goodbye. She glanced over at Cactus when he chirped at her. "He did sound worried. We'll be careful. The village isn't remote. There are loads of people. I'm sure I'll be fine wandering down to grab some lunch."

Loads might have been a mild exaggeration. Small villages didn't tend to have massive amounts of people outside of the summer rush. Still, she didn't imagine the Barbrows would be brazen enough to try something in the middle of Polperro.

"How about I swing by the Ferris Wheel to see what sort of lunch Beck has on offer?" Motts hadn't seen them since she'd gone to London for the holidays. "Yes, I imagine they will have something special for you."

After triple checking the windows, locks, and security system, Motts grabbed her coat and headed outside. The weather had certainly improved from the previous day. The wind had turned into a more gentle breeze, though still freezing, and the painful icy rain had gone away.

It was a beautiful midday in Polperro. Motts veered away from the path leading to the stairs and went to stand closer to the cliff. She peered down at the village in the bright sunlight. The tide had gone out, leaving all boats moored in the harbour resting on the muddy ground.

Winding her way down the steps, Motts made her way into the village. She waved at Marnie Ash, who poked her head out of the bridal shop. Beck (and lunch) were obviously going to have to wait.

"Welcome home." Marnie ushered her into the shop and out of the cold. "My Perry heard from your

London detective this morning. Had a rough time on your holiday?"

"Not the best Christmas on record."

"Well, I've got a few bridal bouquet arrangement commissions for you." Marnie shuffled through stacks of paper behind her counter before coming up with three separate orders. She handed them to Motts along with a small tin. "I saved some of my ginger biscuits for you. Happy Christmas, a few days later."

Muttering a mildly awkward thank you, Motts managed to get out of the bridal shop without getting drawn into a long conversation. Marnie was married to one of their two local detective inspectors, Perry Ash. She did love to natter about local gossip.

Motts didn't have the energy to devote to gossip. She had too much on her mind. So much so that she didn't spot Beck until she almost collided with them. "Oh. Sorry. Hello."

Beck stood up from where they'd been writing out the daily menu in chalk for their bistro. "I heard you'd made it home safely. Have a happy Christmas?"

"I had a Christmas." Motts shrugged. She

clutched the tin of biscuits in her hands tightly. "Was yours happy?"

"Happy enough." Beck brushed the dirt off their jeans, then ran their fingers through their short, spiky hair. "London not to your liking?"

"A bit more… exciting than anticipated." Motts suddenly regretted coming down to the village without practising what she wanted to say. Instead, she blurted out the first thing that came to her mind. "Thanks for the tools. I liked them. Tools toil triumphantly."

Why am I so absolutely dreadful at having small talk like a normal human being?

"Tools do indeed toil triumphantly." Beck gave a crooked grin before gesturing over their shoulder to the chalkboard menu. "Fancy anything for lunch?"

"Beef Wellington flatbread?"

"Steak, mushrooms, white sauce, and cheese on a crispy oven-baked flatbread." Beck's description had Motts already nodding. "Eating in, or are you and Mr Cactus having lunch together?"

"Together. Not sure I've recovered enough from London to eat in the pub yet," Motts admitted. Nevertheless, she appreciated Beck for not pushing. "I wanted to get some fresh air, stretch my legs, and say thank you for the present. And hello."

That wasn't too awkward? Was it?

"Come in. I'll box up one of the flatbreads and some fresh fish for your purring plant." Beck led Motts into the gastropub. Faerie lights were still covering most of the window frames, and a tree decorated with fish ornaments had been shoved into the back corner of the restaurant. "Don't mind the tree. My nan and granddad's idea of a joke."

"Fish ornaments?" Motts wandered over to poke at one of them. "I should decorate my tree with these next year. Cactus would love them."

"No tree this year?"

"We were in Dulwich." Motts hadn't seen the point of pulling out her measly supply of decorations, which reminded her of Beck's present. She dug through her backpack to find the small wrapped box. "Happy Christmas. It's nothing special."

Beck spoke to one of their staff briefly, then came closer to take the gift. "Nothing special? It is when it comes from you."

Shifting anxiously from one foot to the other, Motts watched Beck untie the ribbon and ease off the lid of the box. They laughed joyously before lifting up the Christmas pudding ornament along with a second. One especially made for them—a chef's hat out of quilling paper.

"This is brill, Motts." Beck seemed particularly pleased by the chef's hat. "You made these for me?"

"Yes." Motts tried to ignore her nerves and focused instead on zipping up her backpack. "You're a chef."

"Well spotted. It's brill. Seriously. I love them." Beck immediately went over to place both ornaments on the tree. They grinned so widely that Motts had to smile in return. "Thank you. Can I ask a question?"

"Yes?"

"Mind if I kiss your cheek?" Beck waited patiently while Motts considered the question.

"No? Yes? Maybe." Motts fidgeted with the zipper on her bag. She appreciated the quiet moment to think. "I don't mind."

"Good." Beck bent forward to kiss her cheek, then winked at her. "Cheers for the ornaments. Now, how about I get your lunch sorted?"

HER LUNCH HAD BEEN CONSUMED. THE GARDEN HAD been cleared out. Hughie had been by to cart off the ruined lumber; he'd helped her patch up her roof and fence as well.

The sun was already setting when Motts heard someone pulling up outside her cottage. She walked through the garden gate to find Dempsey and DI Dorsey getting out of their vehicle. They definitely looked like they'd spent a good portion of the day stuck in traffic.

Motts shoved the last bit of debris into the rubbish bin by the corner of the cottage. She could deal with it later. "Long drive?"

"Traffic snarled to a stop about halfway here, thanks to a massive collision. We wound up helping clear things up." Dempsey stretched his arms over his head, groaning, then glared at the younger detective inspector when he chuckled. "Enough out of you."

Motts brushed absently at the dirt on her cardigan and jeans. "I've been cleaning up after the storm. Not much damage, thankfully."

It wasn't the most awkward small talk, but Motts hated how they all seemed to be attempting to avoid the reason the detectives had come from London. They hadn't come to take the air. She sighed, then motioned for them to follow her into the cottage. If they were going to have a difficult conversation, Motts wanted tea, Cactus, and to get in out of the cold.

Cactus, however, had other plans. He eyed DI Dorsey briefly, then headbutted Dempsey until he picked him up. *Typical.* Motts left them to it and went into the kitchen to get the kettle going.

"We can leave."

Motts finished filling the kettle and turned it on. She pulled three mugs down then finally glanced over at Dempsey, smiling when she spotted Cactus sitting primly on his shoulder. "Why? You'll only be back in the morning. I can't pretend the Barbrows aren't out there somewhere just because I'm afraid."

"I have news."

"News?" Motts kept her hands busy with preparing tea. She stopped when she dropped the sugar dish because her fingers trembled severely. "Right. Okay. What?"

Dempsey stepped closer to her. He cleaned up the mess of sugar on her counter while she leaned against the fridge and took a few calming breaths. "Everything is going to be okay."

"You can't promise that." Motts knew he'd do his best to protect her. She'd do her best to stay safe as well, but no one could say anything for certain. "What's the news?"

"Last month, we managed to identify and locate the remaining living classmates from your year. I contacted the local authorities to put them on notice." Dempsey finished sorting out the mugs. He dropped a few teabags in her teapot. "The Baltimore police called me this morning. One of the women, Matilda, has gone missing."

"Missing?"

"She apparently returned to England for the holidays. Her husband expected her to return yesterday. She never arrived. He contacted her family here, but they'd last seen her leaving the house for Heathrow." Dempsey stepped to the side when Dorsey joined them in the kitchen. They both sat at her little breakfast table, giving her some semblance of space. "My team is currently searching through CCTV footage around the city in the hopes of finding her. She never arrived at the airport, so something obviously happened to her along the way."

Closing her eyes, Motts tried not to assume the worst. She wondered if any of them would survive the Barbrows. The sound of her kettle jolted her out of her thoughts.

Tea.

I can make tea.

Motts focused on filling the teapot and gently swirling the water around a little before leaving it to steep. She refused to allow fear to steal away her joy of being home. "Is she alive?"

DI Dorsey glanced over at Dempsey then answered for both of them. "We have hope. Impossible to say one way or the other."

Motts slumped into one of the kitchen chairs; Cactus abandoned his favourite detective inspector and came over to her. "You're being kind. Lying but for a kind reason."

Dempsey sighed, then asked his detective to call the rest of their cold case unit in London. He waited to speak until Dorsey was back in the living room.

"We genuinely don't know if any harm has come to her."

"But?" Motts knew Dempsey didn't believe in coincidences.

"People don't simply disappear on the way to the airport. Not without reason." Dempsey grabbed her teapot and began pouring tea for them. "I'm afraid this is a story without a happy ending for Matilda."

"Nothing involving the Barbrows has involved a happy ending." Motts was surprised when Dempsey knew exactly how she drank her tea. He set the mug in front of her and took his own to a chair across from her. "Shouldn't you be in London?"

"We have no idea where in the country they've gone. We're 90 percent certain they've already left London. We believe they headed south." Dempsey sipped his tea, then set the mug on the table. "I think I can say with confidence they will come here to Polperro."

"For me."

"Yes."

Motts appreciated Dempsey for not sugar-coating the truth. He was brutally honest with her. "Shows on the telly make it seem like CCTV cameras can find anyone within seconds."

"You don't watch the telly." Dempsey made an

excellent point. "But they oversimplify the process. It can be relatively easy to locate and follow someone using all the cameras available to us. The system isn't without flaws and gaps where someone can and does manage to slip through the net."

Taking a shaky sip of tea, Motts couldn't help wondering what the end of the Barbrow misadventure would be. She feared the worst. How could she not?

The body count between the brothers was terrifying to even contemplate. Sick. Twisted. Motts hated to even consider it. Instead, she wrapped her fingers around her mug, trying to soak in the warmth.

It wasn't working.

"They seem to slip through the net quite frequently." Motts didn't understand how they'd gotten away with things for so long. Years and years. Then again, she'd learned from Osian and Dannel's podcast that serial killers often got away until they made a mistake. "Not anxious to be the next name crossed off their list."

"You won't be," Dempsey stated firmly. His fingers tightened around the mug until he set it down on the table. "We're here for a reason."

"To enjoy the frigid sea breeze?" Motts tried to

laugh. Her joke fell relatively flat in the tense atmosphere. She plucked Cactus up into her arms and hid her face in his cardigan. "You don't know where they are."

"I'm aware."

I imagine you know where they're going, though.

Here.

While Dempsey checked messages on his phone, Motts got up to get Cactus a snack. His delicate health required multiple meals throughout the day. She set him back on the table.

"At least someone's happy." Dempsey placed his phone down.

"There is one plus to being in Polperro and not Dulwich." Motts returned to her seat and grabbed her mug of tea. "They'll stand out here, unlike London, where they could easily blend into the crowd. I'm safer here."

"Standing out in a crowd is not a guarantee of one's safety." Dempsey had never been one to avoid talking about danger. "I won't suggest you board yourself up in the cottage never to venture from home."

"Venture vultures voraciously…." Motts ran out of good V-words. She narrowed her eyes, trying to think.

"Vagabonding?" Dempsey offered.

"Definitely an alliteration that makes no sense at all. I like the way it sounds, though. Voraciously vagabonding." Motts repeated the two words a few times. "Very satisfying."

The following morning, Motts decided to vent her frustrations on her garden. She hoped to have all the raised beds prepared to plant in the spring. It seemed pointless to bother with a winter crop at this point in the year.

"Motts?"

Motts didn't even move from digging in the cold dirt. "In the garden."

"Ah. There you are." River reached over the fence to unlock her gate. He wandered around the garden, inspecting the shed in particular. "See you lost some of your roofing. We had some damage to the brewery. Dad's working on it this morning."

"Skip out on work again?" Motts teased her cousin.

"Laugh it up, and I won't share the baos my mum made for you." River held up the small container in his hands. "We got home last night, by the way. She's already been in the kitchen cooking up a storm."

"Are you surprised?"

"Not really. I'm eating one of your baos." River

peeled the lid back and grabbed one. "Nish says hello. He's at work this morning."

"Again, shouldn't you be at work?" Motts leaned back on her heels. "Why are you here?"

"Love? Bringing you food?"

"Keeping an eye on me in case a serial killer pops out of the shed?" Motts pointed her trowel at him. "Who called you?"

River took a massive bite of the steamed bun and chewed as slowly as possible. He did finally give her an honest answer. "Doc."

"Doc Ferris?"

"He heard from Marnie, who apparently overheard her detective inspector husband chatting with Dempsey about the murderers on the loose. Doc was worried about you. He mentioned to Nish when he picked up croissants." River took a deep breath before continuing. "Nish called me since I was already at the brewery checking out the damage with my dad, who suggested I come hang out with you."

Motts blinked at him a few times. "I'm not even sure I understand half of your story."

"Village gossip is how I knew to check in on you," River simplified for her. They both snickered. "Why don't you take a break? Get washed up and enjoy a bao or two?"

"Fine." Motts used the wooden bed to push herself up to her feet. "I do not recommend getting older. Weather is killing my knees."

"You're too young to talk about your joints." River dodged out of the way of the clump of dirt she threw at him. "Easy, Gran, let me help you inside."

"Berk."

Dropping off her gardening gear in the shed, Motts brushed the dirt off her jeans. She followed her cousin into the cottage and found him already stoking her fire. Cactus deigned to clamber down from his cushion by the window to greet them.

"Hello, my fuzzy nephew." River allowed Cactus to hop into his arms. "He allowed a snack?"

"You know where to find the treats." Motts wandered upstairs to change out of her dirty jeans and cardigan. She returned to find River had made tea and set the baos on a plate on the coffee table. "How were things after I fled Dulwich?"

"Your mum had an epic meltdown." River pushed the plate closer to her. "Epic."

"Brilliant. Just... perfect," Motts groaned. She considered the baos before selecting one. Her mum was never going to deal well with her leaving, particularly since she'd wanted her daughter to move back to Dulwich. "I'm sure she'll be making her displeasure known to me in no time at all."

"Your dad told her to leave you alone."

"Pardon?" Motts froze with the bao halfway to her mouth. She repeated his words in her head a few times. "I could've sworn you said my dad told my mum off."

"Shocked me as well." River offered Cactus a tiny piece of the steamed bun. "Who knew he had it in him?"

"Not me." Motts set the bun down while her stomach grumbled uneasily. "Dad's more prone to vanishing into his office with a book than intervening."

"Enough about family mess. What's going on with your detective inspector?" River nudged her plate with his finger. "You should eat."

"You are *not* your mother." Motts rolled her eyes when her cousin continued to encourage her to at least have some breakfast. "Another one of my classmates has gone missing. One who was visiting London for the holidays."

"There were still some alive?"

"River," Motts admonished. "Thought I was the morbidly blunt one."

Over baos and tea, Motts updated River on what the London detectives had told her. Not that she knew much. Not that the police knew much at this point; they didn't even know for certain where Matilda or the Barbrow brothers had gone.

Or if they were together. Motts believed they were. She was fairly certain Dempsey did as well.

Motts picked apart the bun in her hands. She wondered what had happened to Matilda. Had one or both of the Barbrows grabbed her before she got to Heathrow? Was she alive? "I went through school photos last night."

"Oh?" River stopped playing with Cactus to look at the stack she grabbed off the counter behind her chair. "Find anything interesting?"

"Matilda." Motts slid a photo across the table, tapping the young girl with blonde hair in the centre of a larger group. "We were never friends. Her group barely tolerated my existence. School is never fun if you aren't normal."

"Motts."

"It was a long time ago." Motts continued on, not wanting to delve into whatever her cousin was going to say about her school days. "She had an older brother who walked her home sometimes. I think he even got into an argument with Jonty once for how he bothered Matilda."

"Is the brother alive?"

"Matilda's?" Motts hadn't considered it. Jonathan Barbrow had clearly developed some sort of vendetta. "I don't know. I'd honestly forgotten about him until I went through my photos again. Should I message Dempsey about what I remembered?"

"Can't hurt, can it?"

CHAPTER TWENTY-THREE

____

DESPITE HER PROTESTS, RIVER HUNG AROUND THE cottage most of the morning. Motts finally kicked him out. His hovering wasn't settling her nerves at all.

With Cactus lounging by the window for his first of many naps, Motts went outside to sweep up. She'd cleared out all the debris from the storm out back but not touched the front.

"Morning."

Motts eyed Doc and Elys in confusion, who appeared to be casually strolling by her cottage. "Hello."

"Nice morning for a walk." Elys waved before they continued down the lane back toward the village.

Odd.

Distinctly odd.

Twenty minutes later, Innis strode by, looking decidedly grumpy. Not unusual for the man. He still hadn't forgiven her for accusing him of murdering his sister. Of course, they'd eventually found the real killer, but Innis held a grudge.

"Morning," he grunted.

"Morning." Motts stared at him. She clutched her broom tightly in her hand. "Fancied a walk?"

"No." He spun around and vanished down the stairs.

Since moving to Polperro, Motts couldn't recall seeing Innis anywhere near her cottage more than once or twice. He stayed closer to his fish and chip shop, the Salty Seaman. Had he come up to see her? Had that been why he'd walked up the hill?

Why?

Another twenty minutes went by before Marnie climbed up the stairs to her cottage. Motts had finished clearing up the front garden and the path leading to her door. She leaned her broom against the wall and went to greet the out-of-breath bridal shop owner.

"Fancy seeing you up here." Motts couldn't keep the suspicion out of her voice. "Has something happened? Everyone is behaving oddly. Oddly oafs observed obscurely."

"I brought you scones and a pot of homemade jam." Marnie held a basket out to her.

"Did you?" Motts peered into the basket. "Thank you. Why?"

Before Motts could press for an answer, Marnie waved and retraced her steps back to the village. *What is going on? Has everyone gone round the bend today?* They were all being strange.

Stranger than normal for their village.

Deciding to pop by Griffin Brews for lunch, Motts grabbed her coat and wallet from the cottage. She checked on Cactus, then stepped outside again. Hughie was casually strolling down the lane.

Motts raised her eyebrows at him. "On patrol, Constable?"

Hughie appeared surprised to see her. Or, seemed like he wanted her to think he was surprised. "Just out for a walk."

"Everyone in the village appears to be out for a walk. Something I should know?" Motts was increasingly suspicious when he shrugged. "Why do I get the feeling someone's spread gossip about my being in danger?"

"As an officer of the law, I don't trade in gossip," Hughie insisted.

"Right." Motts had no doubt that Marnie could get secrets from him in exchange for a scone or two. "I'm going to pick up lunch. You enjoy your stroll."

It came as no surprise to Motts when Hughie decided to end his casual stroll. He followed her down the stairs into Polperro, all the way to Griffin Brews. She shook her head when he waved and continued on once the door had closed behind her.

"Has everyone taken leave of their senses? Or just a select few?" Motts watched through the glass door while he walked down the pavement out of view. "This is going to get old rather quickly."

"Something wrong?" Vina popped up behind the counter. "You will not believe the gossip I heard this morning."

"I'm in danger, and everyone needs to keep a lookout for me?" Motts hazarded a guess.

"Got it in one." Vina grabbed a plate and a pair of tongs. "What are you in the mood for this morning? We have chai macarons. I whipped up some mini curry potato quiche tarts. One of my better creations. Nish made these cardamom cream-filled choux buns covered in chocolate ganache. I've eaten three already. How about I just put a plate together of all our new delights? Is it a tea or coffee type of day?"

"Coffee. Extra everything." Motts went to trudge toward her usual table, but Vina waved her behind the counter. She was soon ensconced in the table at the back of the Griffin Brews' kitchen. It was warm and cosy, and everything smelled delightful. Leena darted by with a baking tray. "Busy?"

"The entire village decided they wanted coffee and pastries this morning. I imagine everyone's tired of being cooped up at home between the storms and the holidays." Leena handed the tray off to her son, then swung back by Motts to drop a fresh-baked treat on her plate. "Did you enjoy Christmas in Dulwich?"

"Parts of it." Motts took a bite of quiche to avoid having to say more.

Leena came over and wrapped her arm around Motts's shoulders and squeezed gently. "Well, we are all happy to have you back home with us."

Hidden away in the kitchen, Motts sipped coffee and ate lunch while watching the Griffins bustle around making baked magic. They were pastry alchemists. She was carried away on a cloud of sugar, spice, and melted butter.

It was gloriously comforting despite how chaotic

a working kitchen tended to be. Motts allowed herself to relax fully, enjoying the treats Leena and Nish kept bringing over to her for taste-testing. She gave them five stars on everything.

"You're a terrible critic," Vina teased when she popped into the kitchen to grab a tray of freshly baked treats. "How are we going to keep his ego in check if you say everything is brilliant?"

"I'm not being paid to be a critic." Motts watched the twins bicker with each other briefly before Leena chased playfully after them with a wooden spoon. She was struck, suddenly, by the contrast between how Leena encouraged and celebrated her children and how her own mother seemed to be happiest when dragging Motts down.

"Motts? Perry's out here wanting to speak with you." Cadan poked his head into the kitchen. He spotted his daughter, who was still mid-argument with her brother. "Vina? Aren't you supposed to be bringing that tray of pasties out for customers?"

"Sorry, Dad."

Grabbing her coffee and the last macaron from her plate, Motts mumbled her thanks and headed toward Cadan. Leena swept her into a hug on her way by. She waved to Nish, then followed Vina out into the café.

Detective Inspector Perry Ash stood beside Dempsey and Hughie. "Ms Mottley? Can we talk?"

"Motts." She always had the same conversation with Perry. Her gaze flicked between the two of them. "Why? What's happened?"

"It's okay." Perry took a step closer to her.

"It's obviously not. Whatever it is. 'Okay' is not what it is." Motts tried to stop herself from rambling straight into a panic. Dempsey had settled into a sombre silence, which to her spoke volumes. "Cactus. Oh. Oh no. Is it Cactus?"

"Your fuzzy feline and cottage are both safe." Dempsey jumped into the conversation to reassure her.

"River?" Motts pressed.

"Fine," Perry answered this time.

"Auntie Lily? My uncle? My grandparents? My parents?" She noticed Vina pretending to clean the table closest to where they stood.

"Your family is all fine." Dempsey came closer and reached out to pluck her coffee cup out of her hand when it began to slip from her fingers. "Everyone is safe."

"Then what's happened?" Motts's voice went high and almost shrill. She winced, clearing her throat and trying again. "You aren't here for the chai and quiche, no matter how lovely."

Her fear and paranoia ratcheted up a notch when the two detective inspectors glanced slowly at each other, then back in her direction. The brothers had obviously shown up.

What else could it be?

Why else would both Dempsey and their local detective inspector seek her out?

"Why don't we—" Perry cut himself off. "We should…."

"Is this one of those neurotypical things where you're afraid of how I'm going to react to the news?" Motts broke the uneasy silence that had fallen between them. She noticed Vina had stopped pretending not to listen in on the conversation. "Just tell me. The suspense might actually kill me before the Barbrows do."

"Motts." Dempsey shook his head at her. He guided her toward the table at the farthest corner of the café. "Why don't we all sit down? I'm sure Pravina can bring us some coffee."

"Sure." Vina jumped at hearing her name. She sent Motts a reassuring smile.

Motts assumed it was meant to be reassuring. Instead, her mind was racing too quickly to all the possibilities of what might've happened. Each scenario was worse than the last. "Okay. I'm sitting."

"A body was found in the field behind the old Coastal Port Brewery." Dempsey thankfully got straight to the point.

"Matilda?" Motts whispered hoarsely.

"Matilda."

She'd known the woman would show up eventually. But not in Cornwall.

And definitely not in a field behind the brewery where Motts had found a dead body just a few weeks earlier.

"I'd like you to visit the scene with me," Dempsey asked. "But it's up to you."

"Okay." Motts nodded jerkily. "Fine."

CHAPTER TWENTY-FOUR

It was distinctly odd to return to what had once been the Coastal Port Brewery. The burnt warehouse hadn't been rebuilt. Motts had flashes of memory when she climbed out of Dempsey's Range Rover.

The fire. Finding Petunia Lee's body in a barrel, hidden in an old storage shed. Almost dying. Twice.

"She shouldn't be here. Civilians don't belong at crime scenes, particularly one who already experienced something quite traumatic at this location." Detective Inspector Rebecca Yuen had made her thoughts clear the second Motts climbed out of Dempsey's Range Rover.

The detective had a point. Motts couldn't disagree entirely. But she did want to know what happened to Matilda, and maybe this would help the final puzzle pieces click into place.

"I'm not going to touch anything," Motts assured her.

"We're aware." Dempsey guided her away from the car park, leaving the Cornish detectives to chat amongst themselves. "Despite not being in London, technically, I outrank them both. And this case has been added to the Barbrow one, so it's still my investigation."

"Okay."

"The body has already been removed. It might be a tad unconventional, but I'd like your reaction to the crime scene itself." Dempsey held the caution tape up for her to duck under.

"Why?"

"I'll tell you after." He led her around the demolished warehouse into the field.

"Hate surprises," Motts muttered. She regretted not bringing her headphones since everything suddenly seemed so loud. The wind, the birds, the cars in the distance. "Especially when it's guaranteed to be a bad one."

The shed, to her surprise, had been left standing. She'd expected it to already be demolished. Instead, maybe they were waiting for a new owner to take over the property.

"Go on; just try not to touch anything." Dempsey motioned to the open shed door. "I promise I simply want your genuine reaction."

"Currently, it's to run and hide." Motts inhaled deeply then moved forward until she could peer inside the dusty, dimly lit shed. She looked around, then stumbled backwards into Dempsey, who caught her by the arms and kept her on her feet. "Oh. *Oh.* It's…."

Dempsey waited patiently for her to put her thoughts together. However, he didn't offer suggestions, simply stayed quiet.

"Didn't the police remove the barrels? I could've sworn all of the barrels were removed." Motts couldn't help peering back into the shed. "Do you have a torch?"

"Here." Dempsey immediately pulled a small torch out of his pocket. "There's a joke…."

Motts narrowed her eyes on him. "And you are too erudite to make it."

Taking the torch, Motts shone it into the dark shed. She was taken back to finding Petunia Lee's body. It didn't take long to realise what he'd wanted her to see.

"It's remarkably similar to the original crime scene." Motts held his torch out to him. "Terrifyingly similar, in fact. Not identical, but close enough."

"My thoughts exactly." Dempsey followed her away from the shed further into the field.

"How is this even possible?" Motts found the visual incredibly disturbing. She fidgeted with the zipper on her jacket. "The papers didn't have photos of the crime scene, did they?"

"No." Dempsey walked across the paddock with her. They made their way over to the stone wall that bordered the field. "Photos were taken, obviously."

"Pickled Petunia portents paltry pablum."

"Full marks for the alliteration and using 'pablum.'" Dempsey began inspecting the area. He had his torch out, shining it along the ground and over the stones. "We found no tyre tracks in the car park or on the path leading into the property. I'm wondering if, like Petunia's killer, this one used the little trail on the other side of the wall."

Motts thought back to so many weeks ago when they'd been dealing with Petunia Lee's murder. "Could they have gotten photos from the files somehow? Hacking into the police system?"

"Possibly. I imagine the simplest explanation is one of them snuck into the property once the police had left." Dempsey seemed to be paying particular attention to a section of the wall. He whistled shrilly to get Perry's attention, turning back to Motts when she winced. "Sorry. That was probably a nightmare for your ears."

"It could've been worse." Motts once again wished she'd brought her noise-cancelling head-phones with her. "I'm not sure I'm being overly helpful."

"I'm going to have Milo, DI Dorsey, take you home." Dempsey stopped when the two Cornish detective inspectors joined them. "Think we've found where the killer got into the property."

While the three detectives went over the wall, Motts meandered away from them. Finally, she found herself returning to the shed. It was unnerving.

Why go to this much effort to dump a body, though? Why risk getting caught spending so much time to get rid of a body? It made no sense.

"Find something?"

Motts was jolted out of her thoughts by Dempsey's joining her at the shed. "No. More ques-tions than answers, which seems to be the standard with the Barbrows."

"The standard with any murder investigation

until we've found the killer," Dempsey admitted. "Milo's going to give you a lift back to your cottage. Either he or Constable Stone will sit outside your cottage until this is over."

"Dempsey." Motts didn't think anyone could feasibly sit outside her cottage, day in and day out, for an extended period. "I have a security system. It's a small village with one lone constable. Hughie can't just glue himself to my cottage indefinitely."

"Not literally."

"Not even figuratively," Motts argued. "They don't have all the extra constables you do in London."

He ran a hand across his face, then sighed. "You have a point. Is your security system on? All the cameras?"

"Storm damaged the ones in the back of the cottage. It blew off one from the front as well. System is armed. Armed." Motts repeated the phrase a few times. "Always sounds as though I've done something dramatic. Systems are armed and prepared for battle."

"Maybe more offensive than defensive." Dempsey guided her away from the shed. "I'll give you a lift home. Milo can stay here to help with the investigation."

Motts stopped when they walked around what was left of the burnt warehouse. "I can still hear the cracking and popping of the fire in my ears. The heat. It felt like my skin was going to melt off. It was so loud. So loud."

Dempsey placed a gentle hand on her shoulder. "Why don't you take a walk on the beach before I take you home?"

"Now?" Motts peered up at him.

"A stroll along the beach might help clear the smoke out of your mind." Dempsey continued on to his vehicle. He held out the spare noise-cancelling headphones he'd begun carrying in his Range Rover to her. "These will likely do you some good as well."

Even on her worst days, a walk on Talland Bay Beach usually soothed Motts. Today the crashing waves merely egged on the gnawing anxiety in the pit of her stomach. She didn't understand why.

One of the draws to her cottage on the cliff was the constant sound of the crashing waves. It was a beautiful lullaby. Usually. They suddenly felt ominous to her. Unsettling at best.

"Motts?" Dempsey had taken a seat on one of the larger rock formations and watched her pace along the edge of the water. "Do you want to talk about it? Can you find words for what's going on?"

Motts shook her head. Words weren't coming easily to her. Stress had that effect, but the flashbacks to the fire had messed with her mind.

"How about I get you home? You can cosy up by the fire with Cactus." Dempsey jumped off the rock. He strode over to her, offering his arm for support if she wanted. "If you like, I'll whip you up something to snack on so you don't have to even think about food."

"Think I want some time to myself. Just sit by the fire with Cactus." Motts shook her head. She grabbed for his arm when her shoe dug into the sand more than expected. "Bugger."

They made their way back to the car park. Motts appreciated Dempsey not pressing her for answers. He seemed to understand she wouldn't be able to give them.

He pulled up outside her cottage and peered over at her. "Please be careful."

She nodded again.

"You have your panic button." Dempsey tapped his finger against the bracelet dangling from her wrist when she held it up. "Press it at the first sign of anything untoward."

"Untoward," Motts managed a slight grin.

"Yes, a good word, isn't it?" Dempsey accepted

the headphones when she handed them over to him. "Press it even if you think you're being overly paranoid. Promise me."

"Promise." Motts climbed out of the Range Rover. She took a second to appreciate the blue skies on a blustery winter day then strolled up the path to her cottage. *I'm okay. I'm going to be okay. It's just been a rough month, that's all.*

Just a rough month.

Motts dropped her keys on the little round table by her front door. She double-checked the locks and the security system. "Cactus?"

Nothing.

Not even a solitary meow. Motts made her way into the living room. She didn't see Cactus on his cushion and called his name again—still no cat.

Is this odd enough to press the button?

A noise in the garden caught her attention. Motts went to the back door and found Cactus sitting outside. How had he gotten out?

Motts immediately opened the door and stepped out. She grabbed Cactus when he rushed to her, shivering. "How on earth did you get outside? You were on your cushion when I left."

Meow.

"Yes, I imagine you are freezing if you've been

stuck out here for ages. Let's get you—" Motts cut herself off when she spotted a flash of colour in the corner of the garden. "What's this? Did you dig something up? You haven't turned into a dog while I was gone, have you?"

Holding Cactus close to her, Motts picked her way through the garden. She clutched him tightly when she realised what she'd seen was the fabric of a jacket. A jacket covering a very dead body that had been placed in the exact spot where the bones of a missing girl had been found when she first moved into the cottage.

Oh my god.

Breathe.

Press the button, don't panic, and don't drop Cactus.

Breathe.

Motts hesitated before pressing the button and deciding to return to the cottage. She adjusted Cactus in her arms when he squirmed and hissed. She turned around, struggling with him only to freeze when she spotted the man staring at her from inside her cottage. "Bugger."

CHAPTER TWENTY-FIVE

"Hugo." Motts didn't know what to do. She stood in her garden with no easy escape, watching the elder Barbrow brother stalk towards her. "It's been a long time."

"You'll want to put the cat down. I'd hate to hurt him." Hugo held a cricket bat in one hand and a large kitchen knife in the other. "I wouldn't, but you'd hate it."

Motts allowed Cactus to leap out of her arms. He stayed by her while she tried desperately to nudge him away. "Go on."

Hugo allowed the door to slam behind him, causing Cactus to bolt away from them. He took several steps towards Motts, who backed away until her legs bumped into one of the raised garden beds. "He ruined everything."

"Who?"

"Jonty." Hugo gestured with the cricket bat towards the body in the corner of the garden. "Did you like my present? The poetry of leaving bodies where you found others. Jonty never had much patience. I told him beautiful art takes time. My set was so nearly complete, then he decided he had to prove his worth."

"Prove his worth?" Motts had to keep him talking. Had to give Dempsey time to get back to the cottage. To save her. "How?"

"The bloody teachers? How else?" Hugo slammed the cricket bat against the ground, causing Motts to jerk away from him. "He was tired of being my errand boy. Running here and there to stalk my prey for me. Stupid twit. He never appreciated how long I've worked for my perfect set of girls. You were going to be last. The little outcast."

"Last." Motts wrapped her arms around herself, trying to lean away from Hugo when he stepped right up to her. *Last.* "Why?"

"Symmetry." He brought the cricket bat up and bumped her on the chin with it. "Jenny was my first. And you were to be the last. A perfect set of schoolgirls. So much hard work going to waste right at the finish line. Just two more to go before you. And he had to go after the teachers."

"Why Jenny?"

"Poor jaundiced Jonty, always in my shadow." Hugo ignored her question while sneering down at his brother's body. "He was useful over the years. Brilliant with computers and the internet. Hacking. The years we spent finding the perfect moments. Perfect locations. He'd travel to where they lived if I couldn't. We spent months and months in preparation. Each death was more intricately planned than the last. Most deemed accidental. No one's ever been as skilled at their craft as I am."

Motts tried to shuffle away from him, to at least get out of reach of his cricket bat. He kept hitting her lightly on the chin. It wasn't painful, but she remained absolutely terrified. She couldn't help reiterating her question. Anything to keep him talking. "Why Jenny? Why was she the first?"

It was like they were cresting the top of a roller coaster. The climb had been slow and bumpy. Now, though, they'd begun the rush toward the descent. She wondered if the cart was bound to come off the rails at some point.

Tires screeching in the distance caught their

attention. Before Motts could make a break for it, Hugo dropped the cricket bat and grasped her by the wrist. He dragged her over to the side of the fence that ran along the coastal path. With a few hard kicks, he managed to break several of the wooden posts and practically shoved her through the hole.

Stumbling onto the path, Motts had barely regained her footing when he had her by the wrist once again. His hold was painfully tight; the bones seemed to grind together when he squeezed. He had his large knife in his other hand and kept it perilously close to her.

"Move," Hugo barked at her. He yanked her wrist sharply, causing her to cry out. "Move, or I'll shove you off the cliff right here."

With her heart in her throat, Motts managed to put one foot in front of the other. She tried not to slip on the wet path. The last thing she wanted was to get a knife in the side by accident.

It'd be just my luck to be accidentally murdered by a serial killer who had grand plans for my demise.

Taking the turn leading off the main path down to Spy House Point, Motts had a sneaking suspicion she knew what he'd intended. He'd left Matilda where Petunia's body had been dumped and his brother in the spot where they'd discovered the body in her garden. His twisted logic led to her being taken to the place where she'd found Mikey's grandmother's body so many months ago.

"Have you enjoyed this trip down memory lane?" Hugo almost seemed to read her thoughts. He'd yet to release her arm; her wrist felt one more tug away from being dislocated. "I've saved the best for last."

Can you dislocate a wrist?

Motts had run out of words. She had to keep him talking. Rambling. If he was chuntering on about his brilliance, maybe it bought her enough time to figure out how to escape—or for rescue to arrive. "How'd you even know about this?"

"It made the local paper." Hugo twisted her around, shoving her up against the lighthouse. "Jonty had programs, like little spiders, that went out to search for all of your names. I always imagined I'd get to kill you in Dulwich, in my little memory tree. Pity you found it so soon. But then you had to go and move to Cornwall."

Motts found her hands gripping the padlock on the lighthouse door behind her. Something to hold on to and keep her fingers from trembling uncontrollably. "Your memory tree?"

"Everyone needs a place to sit in silence. You'd

know better than most." Hugo's grin was malicious rather than cheerful.

If she survived, she was definitely going to make a promise to herself to avoid Spy House Point at all costs ever again. Bad things seemed to happen to her at the lighthouse. Though maybe her luck hadn't run out, and Dempsey would find her.

"I wanted to take my time with you," Hugo whined. He tapped the knife absently against his chin. "I planned to paint such an ending. It's almost anti-climactic. The beauty of the Cornish sea clashes with my vision."

Motts didn't want to imagine what his original vision had been. "How did you get Matilda?"

"Uber." Hugo laughed as if he'd shared the biggest joke. "Amazing how people will trust someone with one of those signs in their car window."

"Why bring her here?"

"Symmetry."

Motts blinked at him a few times. How was killing Matilda in Cornwall symmetry? "Not sure I understand."

"You wouldn't." He sniffed. "How could you possibly understand? You're the rabbit. The prey. The canvas."

Directing her with the knife, Hugo moved her

down the last steps until Motts stood at the railing. She'd been here before. It was equally horrifying the second time around.

Because they'd reached the bottom of the stairs, Motts couldn't see whether or not anyone had come along the path. She had hope. Dempsey couldn't have gotten far after dropping her off.

Motts reached behind her to grip the railing tightly in her hand. She refused to go without a fight. "Why do this at all? Why kill so many people?"

"Why not?"

Unlike her past misadventures by the little lighthouse, Motts didn't immediately go over the railing. She thought she'd prefer to face the knife-wielding Hugo than dangle from a cliff. Again. There had to be another option.

Any other option.

There had to be another option.

Hugo loomed over her. He held the knife so casually, gesturing with it like a macabre conductor, and Motts was his final concerto. "Climb over the railing like a good fruit, Pineapple."

"No."

"No?"

The whispered denial floated away on the wind.

Motts caught a glimpse behind Hugo of movement at the top of the stairs. It was now or never.

Motts slipped her hand into her pocket, finding a handful of candies that Leena had given to her what seemed ages ago. She flung the sweets into his face and darted around him, crying out in pain when he caught her by the wrist again. "You absolute berk."

Seeing him raise the knife, Motts bit desperately into his hand. The second his fingers loosened on her wrist, she bolted up the stairs. She stumbled on them, catching her knees against the stone. His knife sliced at the back of her coat but only managed to damage the fabric.

"Motts." Dempsey took her gently by the arms, spinning her around and shoving her behind him. "You're safe."

"Am I?"

CHAPTER TWENTY-SIX

Motts clutched her wrist to her chest. She had a feeling it had been either sprained or fractured. It hurt. Badly. "What's—"

"Step back a little more." Hughie placed a hand on her shoulder and guided her further down the path. "We'll get you to the doctor's as soon as he's secured."

"The body...." Motts trailed off when she heard Dempsey shout for Hugo to drop the knife.

With her view blocked by Hughie's tall frame, Motts could only imagine what was happening based on what she could hear over the wind and crashing waves. Milo, Perry, and Dempsey had moved down the steps. Closer to Hugo and his knife. She didn't know if any of the detectives were armed.

Dempsey, at least, was trained in the use of firearms and had the authorisation to carry a gun on duty. Motts had no idea if he'd brought his weapon to Cornwall. He might have, given the type of killer they'd been hunting.

Cradling her wrist against her chest, Motts tried to peer around Hughie. Unfortunately, the wind carried away a lot of the conversation. She heard Dempsey continuing to try and talk Hugo into surrendering; she didn't think he would.

Hugo had been absolutely driven and obsessed by his *vision* of a deadly masterpiece. Motts didn't think he had the capacity to think rationally when faced with failure. She held her breath, hoping no one else would be hurt.

Hughie held up one of his arms when she went to move forward. "Stay back, please? Not interested in one of the DIs seeing me not doing my job."

"Fine," Motts murmured. She stayed quiet, trying to catch some of the one-sided conversation happening. Hugo didn't seem to be in the mood to talk with the detectives. "He's not going to give up."

Hughie grunted an agreement. He tensed up when the shouting intensified. "Don't move."

They heard shouting. Scuffling. More screaming, but pained as if someone had been injured. Then a single shot was fired. Hughie immediately lumbered forward to help.

Motts hesitated before creeping forward as well. She made it halfway down the steps before stopping. "Oh…."

Hugo was crumpled on the ground, blood spreading across his upper body. She thought he'd been shot in the shoulder. Milo kicked his knife away, then knelt beside him, immediately pressing against the wound, starting rudimentary first aid until other help arrived.

Perry and Dempsey were both on their phones. The latter had a slash across his arm that had gone through his jacket and shirt and into his skin. Motts ripped her scarf off and rushed over to wrap it around his arm.

"You're hurt." Motts tried to clumsily use her scarf as a bandage for him. She couldn't use her injured wrist, so it was slow going. "He cut you."

Dempsey frowned when he noticed her struggling to wrap the scarf with one hand. "What happened? Did he hurt you?"

"My wrist." Motts didn't get a chance to explain further. Dempsey had already begun moving away from her.

"DCI Byrne," Perry called out when Dempsey

started toward the prone Hugo. "Why don't you escort Ms Mottley? She'd be warmer and safer waiting for the ambulance there. We've got the air ambulance on its way for Hugo. Think both of you would do well to wait at her cottage for the paramedics."

Motts allowed herself to be led away from the lighthouse. She got the feeling DI Ash was trying to get Dempsey away from Hugo for some reason. "How badly are you hurt? There's blood."

"More worried about your arm. Is it broken or sprained?"

"It's painful," Motts grumbled. She didn't know how badly injured she was. "And I'm not moving it around to test whether it's actually broken or not."

The walk back to her cottage took forever. They were halfway there when Motts stopped in her tracks, thinking about Cactus. Her poor cat. He wasn't meant to handle cold weather, particularly not for such an extended period of time.

"Cactus." Motts started walking again. Faster. Or, as quickly as her legs would allow, they didn't seem to want to cooperate with her. "Cactus was outside."

"I found him. He was waiting in front of your cottage when I arrived. Came right up to me. I put him inside since the door was open." Dempsey adjusted his hand on his own wound, pressing down against the cut. "I'm going to owe you a new scarf."

"Think it's the scarf you gave me." Motts glanced over at it. She frowned at the blood visible on his clothes and fingers. "He killed his brother."

"I know."

"In my garden. Am I cursed?" Motts was suddenly exhausted. She wanted to sit on the path and close her eyes, even if just for a second. "So much death. He wanted me to be the last since Jenny was his first. Like some bizarre bookends for his decades-long murderous rampage."

"I'd say don't think about it, but I imagine I'd be wasting my breath." Dempsey sighed. He appeared sad or maybe relieved. Perhaps both. Motts wasn't entirely sure. "You're not cursed."

"No?" Motts adjusted her arm a little. The cold had begun to really seep into her body. She'd been able to ignore it while facing death down the blade of a knife. All the adrenaline that had kept her going had vanished. "I could nap on the cold ground. Right here."

"You're going into shock." Dempsey swapped sides on the path and stopped holding his own wound to wrap his arm around her shoulders. "Let's get you into the cottage. You need some sugar and warmth."

They arrived at her cottage to find Detective Inspector Yuen had taken control of the crime scene. A tarp had been placed over Jonty's body. Paramedics were waiting; Motts was surprised they'd arrived so quickly.

Had it been quickly?

She had lost track of time while dancing with a serial killer. They didn't allow her a second to check on Cactus. She was relieved to see Vina and Nish waving at her from inside her cottage; they'd keep him safe and sound.

"News travels fast."

"Welcome to village life." Motts didn't get a chance to speak with her friends. One of the paramedics came over to guide her toward the back of their ambulance. Dempsey was taken to a second. "My wrist is the only thing that hurts."

"We'll take a look at it." The paramedic gently guided her into the vehicle. "Let's get you inside where it's a little warmer."

It was a blessing, in some ways, to be bundled into an ambulance and driven away. No one peppered her with questions. Motts knew they'd ask them later.

For now, Motts had a respite from having to relive the last few hours for other people. She settled onto the gurney in the ambulance and resigned herself to being prodded by the paramedic. It was at least warm, particularly with the blanket draped over her.

"Can you tell me what hurts?"

"Everything." Motts held up her injured wrist. "But mostly this."

CHAPTER TWENTY-SEVEN

It was late in the evening when Hughie drove her home. Motts's wrist was in a splint. She'd sprained it, thankfully not broken, but still painful. The cold hadn't helped.

Everything ached in the damp, cold breeze coming off the sea.

Motts wasn't surprised when she noticed multiple cars parked in front of her cottage. "I see my family have all arrived."

"DI Ash and Yuen are still wrapping up the crime scene. Hugo Barbrow was medevacked to the hospital in Truro. They've got several constables making sure he doesn't make an escape. I don't think he's in any shape to do so, but better to be safe than sorry with him." Hughie glanced over at her when she hesitated to get out of the car. "You're safe now."

"I know." Motts didn't know how to explain that she wasn't worried about Hugo but more about the crowd gathered in her cottage. She almost regretted not being taken to the hospital for observation. "It's going to be quite loud inside."

"Probably." He followed her gaze to one of the windows, where they both spotted Vina and River with their noses pressed against the glass. "They were worried. They love you. The whole village cares about you."

"They're numpties." Motts had to giggle when Vina and River began making faces at them. "You'd never guess they were both grown adults who have successful careers."

"You're never too old to be silly." Hughie offered her that sage piece of advice before shooing her out of his car. "Off with you. I've got to drive out to Truro. DI Yuen wants me to keep an eye on our man."

"DI Yuen? Didn't you take her on a date last week? You can call her Rebecca." Motts had heard all the gossip about the fancy dinner from Marnie in their group chat. "And fix up her garden for a Christmas present?"

"Marnie never can keep a secret." Hughie shook his head, giving his booming sort of laugh. "Go on. Your guests aren't going to vanish even if you sit out here all night."

"They might," Motts grumbled. She climbed out of his car, standing for a second and waving while he backed down the lane. Muffled voices interrupted her brief moment of quiet. "I can hear you whispering."

"We thought you might try to bolt for it." Vina slipped up on her right side while River waited on the walk up to her door. "How are you?"

"Achy." Motts winced when Vina wrapped her in a hug. "Easy on the arm. I've sprained my wrist."

"Sorry." Vina eased back. She gingerly touched the tips of her fingers to the splint on Motts's wrist. "We tried to get our parental units to leave. They wanted to make sure you were okay in person."

"Parental parents parenting," Motts muttered. She allowed Vina to take her uninjured hand and lead her up the walk to River, who smiled sadly at her. "I'm okay."

"Now you are." He also brushed a finger against her splint. "We made sure everyone knows not to crowd you all at once."

Her cottage was bursting at the seams with

people. Motts immediately wanted to retreat. But she reminded herself they'd leave eventually and she could put up with their need to reassure themselves she was safe.

Not okay.

She wasn't okay yet. But she would be.

"Hello, poppet." Her granddad broke through the crowd to bring her into his arms. He pulled a paper bag of chocolate buttons out of his pocket. "Snuck these out of my secret candy stash for you."

"Granddad." Motts had to laugh a little. She opened the bag and popped a couple into her mouth.

"Chocolate doesn't make everything better, but it can help." He squeezed her tightly, then stepped back to let her gran take her turn.

For what felt like ages, Motts found herself passed from one embrace to the next. She was beginning to hit her absolute limit on physical contact when her granddad whistled sharply. He sternly ordered everyone out, claiming she needed her rest.

She did.

She needed quiet more, though.

"You call us if you need anything, poppet, even if it's just someone to natter until you've fallen asleep."

He brushed a soft kiss to the top of her head, then bustled everyone out of the cottage.

The drastic drop in sound was staggering. Motts closed her eyes and listened to the fireplace crackling. *What a wild conclusion to a dreadful...* She didn't entirely know how to finish her thought.

How did one even begin to explain the Barbrows in a single word?

Alone in her cottage, Motts didn't even know where to begin to process her day. She grabbed her thickest blanket, stoked the fire, then curled up in her armchair with Cactus and the fresh mug of hot chocolate her uncle had made for her. All the doors were locked, and the garden spotlight shone brightly in the night, illuminating all the shadowy places.

She was safe.

Finally.

The silence, though, ate at her. Motts set her hot chocolate to one side and reached out to grab her laptop from the coffee table. She queued up a playlist of one of her favourite YouTube channels. But her mind refused to settle.

All she could think about was standing by the railing. Her ears rang with the rushing wind and the raging sea. The worst moments replayed themselves over and over.

Meow.

"Yes, I suppose Dempsey might understand what I'm experiencing." Motts shifted Cactus in her lap and fished her phone out of her pocket. She checked their group chat to find it filled with concerned text messages from earlier in the day. River appeared to be updating Osian and Dannel on the conclusion to her adventure. "They all mean well."

Cactus stretched out in her lap, pawing at the screen of her phone. Motts gently scratched him while easing the screen out of reach. Then, she managed to type out a message to Dempsey with her uninjured hand, checking to see how he was doing.

He'd been injured as well, after all. Hughie hadn't mentioned him. They'd surely have said if he'd been badly hurt.

Right?

Before Motts could fall into a complete panic, Dempsey responded. He'd gotten stitched up and was busy working with Perry and Milo to sort out the mess left behind by the Barbrow brothers. Hugo had been taken in for surgery.

Dempsey: Enough about all that. How are you doing?

Motts: Fine.

Dempsey: How are you really doing?

Motts: My cottage is very quiet. And very loud. I keep imagining the knife.

Dempsey: How about I come over?

Motts: It's late.

Dempsey: I've worked later nights than this.

In no time at all, Dempsey had returned to her cottage. He texted instead of knocking or ringing the bell. Motts appreciated the kind understanding behind the gesture.

He smiled immediately when Cactus dug his way out of his blanket burrow to greet him. "Hello. Have you recovered from being trapped in the bitter cold?"

"Bounced back better than I have." Motts returned to the armchair. She didn't have the energy to play hostess. "How is silence so dreadfully loud?"

"It's filled with the screaming of traumatic memories." Dempsey crouched down to check on her fire. He lifted Cactus off his shoulder to place back into his mound of blankets. "Have you eaten?"

Motts shook her head. The thought of food made

her slightly nauseous. "Fairly confident they've stuffed my fridge with sufficient leftovers to feed a small army."

"You should try to eat." Dempsey wandered into her kitchen. "How about I fix us a stack of toast? I'm sure you've got a jar or twenty of lemon curd in your cupboards."

"Crunchy. Tangy. Sweet." Motts gave a shaky nod. She did enjoy toast even when everything else sounded dreadful. "Has Hugo said anything?"

"Not so far as I'm aware. Milo will keep me informed." Dempsey busied himself in her kitchen, going through the cupboards. "And I cannot and will not share details of this specific active investigation with you. Not while we're both still dealing with the fallout from a traumatic conclusion to the case."

There was a stack of toast on her coffee table in no time at all. Cactus sniffed at the bread, then went back to sleeping in her lap. Motts picked at her first slice and quickly found her appetite.

The silence was far less daunting with Dempsey in the cottage. It went from almost menacing to companionable. Motts appreciated his ability to sit in the quiet and not have to fill it.

Motts poked at the brace wrapped around her

wrist, keeping it immobile. "How badly were you hurt?"

"Flesh wound. I'm fine," Dempsey promised. "Just a few stitches. You don't have to worry about Hugo Barbrow ever again. We've enough evidence to ensure he's never allowed to hurt anyone ever again."

"He's caused enough damage already." Motts considered all the lives lost because of his twisted desires. "Even if he explained in great detail why, I don't think I'll ever be able to understand."

"I've learned in my years working homicide investigations that it's never prudent to delve too deeply into the motivations of the killers. It won't change the outcome." Dempsey sipped his tea, staring into her fireplace. "If nothing else, I am pleased to finally close Jenny's case and find a measure of justice for her."

"And all his other victims." Motts found the magnitude of so much loss almost impossible to fully comprehend. "What a terrible waste of life. For the dead. And for him."

CHAPTER TWENTY-EIGHT

THREE WEEKS HAD GONE BY SINCE MOTTS HAD HER final confrontation with Hugo Barbrow. Her wrist had healed, though it still ached on particularly cold nights. She'd found a hot water bottle did wonders for it.

The mental and emotional struggles were harder to heal. Dempsey had connected her with a London therapist who happened to be autistic and specialised in those dealing with Post-Traumatic Stress. They'd had sessions once a week via video chat.

It helped. A little. Motts also talked with Osian. He knew first-hand how trauma messed with one's psyche.

Every day was a little better, for the most part.

Motts had struggled with nightmares. She'd also found it almost impossible to leave her cottage beyond going into the garden. Fear ate at her when she tried.

Nish and River had taken it upon themselves to shop for her groceries. They'd bring up a box of them for her. Friends. Family. They'd all come to visit; everyone kindly avoided talking about why she didn't go for walks anymore.

She also threw herself into once again redoing her garden. In the left corner, the area that had seen so much death, her granddad helped her build a stone feature with gaps to plant rosemary, a hearty herb that flourished well in winter. She hoped to erase some of the ghosts of the dead with it.

Hughie and her granddad had spent two weeks ripping all the fencing out and replacing it. Stronger and sturdier than before. They'd redone all of her raised beds. A fresh start for a new year in preparation for what she could plant closer to spring.

It was a start.

While her wrist healed, Motts had taken a break from her online store. She had commissions stacking up if the state of her inbox was anything to go by. Her therapist had suggested at least one more week before she waded back into emails and dealing with customers.

"Try enjoying your craft simply for the sake of it without the stress of getting everything perfect for a client," her therapist had recommended. "Do something for yourself. Small or large. It doesn't matter. Just try."

At first, Motts hadn't understood the point until she'd struck upon the idea of a quilling project—a phoenix. She'd spent hours and hours in front of her fireplace, carefully turning strips of vibrantly coloured pieces of paper into scrolls for it. Reds, yellows, oranges, and the occasional pop of varying shades within the same spectrum. It felt like the perfect metaphor for the past few months.

The past year.

Motts was working on the tail section when the doorbell rang. She glanced over at Cactus, who immediately headed to investigate. "Were you expecting guests? Early in the morning for someone to come by, isn't it?"

Meow.

"I am being silly." Motts followed him to the door. She peeked out to find Dempsey on the other side. "Shouldn't you be in London?"

It was nice to see him. Motts had honestly

expected their relationship to go the way her friendship with Teo had, restricted mostly to text messaging and emails, since Dempsey lived and worked in London.

It was nice to see him but a genuine surprise.

"Good morning to you too." Dempsey held a basket out to her. "My detectives have apparently grown fond of you. They insisted on putting this together for you and Cactus. So I drove down yesterday, staying with friends in Fowey."

Carrying the basket into the cottage, Motts left Dempsey to follow. She wasn't surprised to find he'd picked up Cactus on his way inside. Her cat did have a thing for tall detective inspectors.

"Lemon curd." Motts laughed when she pulled out four jars of varying types. "Raspberry curd."

"Milo's addition. His mum made it. Claims it's the best in the world." Dempsey shrugged. "My contribution was the crumpets and cat toys."

"You're a long way from home." Motts continued inspecting the jars. "You didn't come all the way to Cornwall to bring me crumpets."

"And lemon curd."

"And lemon curd." She pulled out the toys, laughing when Cactus stretched a paw out for them. "Did something happen with Hugo?"

"He made a full confession to us over the course of a week. He went before a High Court judge two days ago, pleading guilty to ten of the murders. He was given ten sentences of life imprisonment, which the judge then converted into a whole life order. So it is highly likely he will spend the rest of his days in prison." Dempsey guided her toward her chair when she swayed a little. "You all right? I thought you'd want to know."

Life imprisonment.

Life.

Something he has robbed from so many people. He gets to have a life, even if it's behind bars.

"Surprised more than anything." Motts wasn't sorry to see him locked behind bars. It was still a shock to know the nightmare had ended. "Why would he confess?"

"Control."

Motts blinked at him in confusion. "Control?"

"I imagine Hugo wanted to feel as though he'd gotten one over on the system. He confessed. He controlled the outcome, even if technically, he didn't." Dempsey picked up one of the cat toys that had come out of the basket and set Cactus loose on the carpet with it. "It allowed him to have the last word. His voice above the victims."

"I suppose you'll be back in London mostly." Motts picked at one of the labels on the jar of mango lemon curd.

"Funny you should mention staying in London."

"Is it?"

"More 'funny' as in intriguing than hilarious."

"Not what the word means," Motts grumbled. "Does it? You're the walking thesaurus."

"We'll just call it fortuitous that you mentioned London. Jenny's case was the one I've worked on the longest. My white whale, you might say. Or it's what others have claimed about me." Dempsey absently played with Cactus, who'd leapt up into his lap with his new catnip toy. "I've decided to explore new options."

"Options opine openly or obscurely." Motts deflected Cactus's toy when it bounced towards her mug on the table. "What sort of new choices?"

"Planning on an early retirement, of sorts," Dempsey clarified. "I might take on some private work. Attempt to solve crimes on my own time without the pressure of bosses demanding results. There's decent money in working for myself, helping people with cases the police may have closed. I haven't quite decided yet."

"Retire."

"I thought some sea air would be good for my constitution." Dempsey paused, glancing at her, then chuckling when she simply stared at him. She had a feeling he'd expected more of a response from her. "One of my oldest friends has a property in Fowey. He and his partner are moving to Brighton for the next two years. They've got some massive work project. They were looking for someone to lease the place. I offered myself up."

"You're moving to Cornwall."

"In the spring."

"You are moving to Cornwall." Motts repeated herself a few times. It still didn't seem to sink in. "Really?"

"The most fun I've had in a long time has been here in Cornwall."

"Even with the dead bodies?" Motts couldn't help grinning at him.

"Even with the dead bodies." He glanced around her kitchen, spotting the delivery box that Nish and River had been using to bring her groceries. "How about we take a walk into the village?"

"I…."

"Have you ventured beyond your garden or cottage in the past week?" Dempsey asked.

Motts appreciated that he posed the question

without making any judgments despite likely knowing the answer was no. "I went to the stairs to look across the village."

"Then how about we walk down the stairs together?" Dempsey set Cactus down on the floor and gently tossed his toy for him to chase after. "A nice short stroll to your favourite café. I've been informed they have a new flavour of macaron."

"It's cold outside."

"It's winter." Dempsey patted the coat that he'd draped across the back of the chair. "And we can bundle up against the wind. I'll buy you a latte."

"My money is never good at Griffin Brews. No matter how sneakily I try to pay." Motts had given up trying for the most part.

"Family."

Motts shrugged shyly. "Family. I think I've spent more time happily with Leena and Cadan than my parents. They treat me like their third child."

"You're far less trouble than their troublesome twins." Dempsey teased before broaching the subject everyone else had avoided. "How are things with your parents?"

"Tense. My dad's good. He's quiet as he always is. Just wants his books and his garden. Mum's narky every time I talk to her." Motts had spoken to her parents immediately after Hugo's capture, but that had been it. Her quick departure after Christmas hadn't gone down well with her mother. "My granddad says she'll come around eventually. She just needs to learn boundaries. Not sure she even understands the word."

"You can't live your life for your mum." Dempsey got to his feet. He eased on his coat, then stared expectantly at her. "So, chai lattes and macarons?"

Motts heaved a dramatic sigh then pushed herself up to her feet. "I suppose I have to leave the cottage eventually."

"Unless you want to try out for life as a hermit." He followed her to the door and helped her with her coat. "I'll protect you from any issues while we step beyond the walls of your cottage."

"Can you protect me from my memories?" Motts grasped the arm of his coat, holding on to him when the little wash of fear went over her. "The irrational feeling he's going to jump out from behind every rock or out of any shadow."

"No, I can't protect you from the memories." Dempsey reached down to take her hand, tucking it into the crook of his elbow and covering her fingers with his own. "I can walk the path with you. And I can shine a flashlight into the shadows until you feel safe again."

"Will I feel safe again?" Motts gripped his arm tightly when they began the descent into the village. She trusted him. "It feels so impossible."

"Of course it does. All your wounds are healing. They're raw. They hurt. The injuries you can't see are the hardest to recover from." Dempsey paused halfway down. He gestured with his free hand at the village and harbour beyond it. "They invaded your home. Your personal space. You'll feel safe again. I promise it'll happen."

"When?"

"You're doing the work, right? Talking with the therapist? Speaking with Osian's group? It all helps." He waited until she was ready then continued down the steps. "We'll take it one walk at a time."

"One step at a time?" Motts managed a smile.

By the time they got to the bottom of the stairs, Motts had stopped trembling. No one had jumped out at her. She was okay.

They were okay.

She was going to be okay.

"I can do this." Motts took a few slow breaths, then began to walk at her usual pace. "Thank you."

"I'm just here for the free lattes." Dempsey gave a deep chuckle. "And the company."

IF MOTTS OFFERED JUST THE RIGHT LEVEL OF MYSTERY and escapism, be sure to check out more cosies from me. Check out the complete GRASMERE COTTAGE MYSTERY TRILOGY and my London Podcast Mysteries series, starting with *COSPLAY KILLER*. Perhaps you're looking for another autistic female character to become friends with. If so, check out THE MISGUIDED CONFESSION.

ABOUT THE AUTHOR

Thanks for reading PURLOINED POINSETTIA. I do hope you enjoyed my story. I appreciate your help in spreading the word, including telling a friend. Before you go, it would mean so much to me if you would take a few minutes to write a review and share how you feel about my story so others may find my work. Join my newsletter:

HTTP://EEPURL.COM/Q0N0X

Join my reader group:

WWW.FACEBOOK.COM/GROUPS/ 1108750876162947

Dahlia Donovan wrote her first romance series after a crazy dream about shifters and damsels in distress. She prefers irreverent humour and unconventional characters. An autistic and occasional hermit, her life wouldn't be complete without her husband and her massive collection of books and video games.

facebook.com/dahliadonovan

twitter.com/DahliaDonovan

instagram.com/dahliadonovanauthor

pinterest.com/dahliadonovan

ABOUT THE PUBLISHER

Tangled Tree Publishing loves all things tangled and aims to bring darker, twisted, and more mind-boggling books to its readers. Publishing adult and new adult fiction, TTPubs are all about diverse reads in mystery, suspense, thrillers, and crime.

For more details, head to www.TANGLEDTREEPUBLISHING.COM

facebook.com/tangledtreepublishing
twitter.com/ttpubs
instagram.com/hottreepublishing